Kierkegaard's Clown

Kierkegaard's Clown

A Novel

Jerome Donovan

iUniverse, Inc.
New York Lincoln Shanghai

Kierkegaard's Clown
A Novel

Copyright © 2007 by Jerome Donovan

iUniverse books may be ordered through booksellers or by contacting:

iUniverse
2021 Pine Lake Road, Suite 100
Lincoln, NE 68512
www.iuniverse.com
1-800-Authors (1-800-288-4677)

Because of the dynamic nature of the Internet, any Web addresses or links contained in this book may have changed since publication and may no longer be valid.

This is a work of fiction. All of the characters, names, incidents, organizations, and dialogue in this novel are either the products of the author's imagination or are used fictitiously.

ISBN: 978-0-595-44012-2 (pbk)
ISBN: 978-0-595-68476-2 (cloth)
ISBN: 978-0-595-88333-2 (ebk)

Printed in the United States of America

For my family

Reunion in The Gambia

Reza Krishen and I hang on grimly as the dilapidated pickup truck from Rough & Ready Tours of The Gambia lurches and rolls down the rutted dirt road through the wilting fields of vegetables and peanuts. We face each other in the back of the truck on two worn wooden benches extending lengthwise from the cab to the tailgate, struggling to keep our knees from touching, like self-conscious schoolboys on a backcountry outing.

It is nearly noon. The sky is low and leaden, and the soul-wilting humidity has already sucked all vitality from us, like a paper towel passing over a damp countertop. We have arranged this weekend excursion to temporarily escape our boredom—the familiar and predictable ennui that inevitably extinguishes the enthusiasm of any visitor to this place, especially that of visiting Westerners like us. We are here to help the Gambians but can barely muster the energy to even rouse ourselves.

The Gambia—in a touching attempt to retain some token of postcolonial dignity, the government insists on the "The"—is a tiny English-speaking sliver of sand, scrub land, and mangrove swamps on Africa's Atlantic coast, hemmed in on three sides by French-speaking Senegal. Reza and I are independent consultants on a two-week assignment for the American international development agency, USAID, to investigate prospects for expanding the country's agricultural production beyond its historic dependence on peanuts. As the team's lawyer, my official task is to assess how to change Gambian laws to accommodate this ambitious new policy. We will fly home in seven days.

Unofficially, I am here to persuade the government to take the political and practical steps—in which I will helpfully instruct them—to implement several other changes in its agricultural policies that the U.S. government prescribes for all such poor countries. I am well aware that these changes will expose The Gambia's small-scale farmers to America's agribusiness giants and their mass-production techniques, including their dangerous theories on genetically modified crops. Like America's family farms before them, The Gambia's intimate farming culture, the keystone to its very way of life, is to be swept into the thresher of Western agribusiness.

My job is to convince the Gambians that this will be a good thing; this will be progress. Of course, no officials or farmers will believe me. They will see my prepackaged orthodoxies for what they are—self-serving heresies issuing from some faraway and alien power. From the standpoint of my employers my mission will succeed only if the Gambian officials, in an unsentimental calculation, conclude that the benefits to themselves of my proffered solutions outweigh the certain damage to their peoples' lives.

Reza is tall, fit, and graying, a sixty-five-year-old agronomist from Kerala, in southwestern India. He is a "St. Thomas Catholic," an heir to the Christian branch that the Apostle Thomas—"Doubting Thomas"—founded in his post-Resurrection travels to the East. But I have never seen in Reza the spiritual fervor that I have always associated with Indians. Indeed, to me he typifies the familiar suave, fully assimilated Third Worlder—someone who has, chameleon-like, so thoroughly acquired the hues of his comfortable Western perch that he and his perch are now indistinguishable from one another.

I am a stocky, quiet (some say borderline surly), forty-two-year-old divorced lawyer from northern California. I went to U.C. Berkeley's law school and endured four years of a dull general practice in Petaluma before taking my first interesting legal job, advising Honduras on certain aspects of a so-called free-trade agreement with the United States. A law school classmate working in Washington threw the assignment my way.

Reza and I have been in The Gambia for just a week and have immediately slipped into the familiar pattern. We lodge in the country's best hotel, high above the once-broad beaches from which the government has gouged thousand of tons of sand for use in construction projects. For every high-rise tourist condominium the government has built with the sand, probably two condominiums' worth of tourists have avoided The Gambia because of its vanishing beaches.

Frequently our previously scheduled meetings with ministers and other officials are abruptly cancelled without explanation. So we pass most of our days drinking in a semi furtive fashion and eating long lunches by the pool. When we work at all, it is in our respective rooms, typing our "deliverable"—our assignment's report—into our laptops, a task we began two weeks before leaving home.

Overall, our routine is sweaty and desultory. We begin the day with an acceptable level of energy and efficiency. But after an hour or two, it invariably deteriorates to a lethargic, dogged determination to squeeze just enough of the standard, limp prose into the "deliverable's" rigid format. We stay the required number of days and then bolt on the first available flight.

Now not even the whining, jarring lurching of our small official "tourist truck" can keep me fully awake. I am vaguely on the lookout for bargains—local crafts to add to the closetful of almost identical stuff I have in my Maryland house. It is stuff I seldom look at but think that my grandchildren—if I ever married again and had children—would sort through at my death and, in their loving ignorance, perhaps think of me as a savvy connoisseur of native artifacts.

Where the fields border the road, spiky bushes vie for space with ten-foot-high termite mounds. Shaggy-barked trees, ranging in height from three to thirty feet, block our view of the fields themselves, a forbidding display of arboreal aggression, probably required to repel the voracious local termites.

In the distance, through gaps in the trees, we can see local women weeding their vegetable patches in stately slow motion. Most of these women carry sleeping infants on their backs; the infants bound to their mothers' backs with lengths of brightly colored cloths, in the timeless manner of rural poverty, fusing the mundane and the maternal from the baby's birth to its mother's death.

Hearing our truck approach, the women straighten up and turn toward us, and we wave to them. They smile in their resigned and languid manner and wave back. They seem genuinely pleased to see us.

I sometimes wonder if these women ever tire of playing unpaid roles in the government's efforts to promote this kind of "ecotourism," if they ever tire of waving to foreigners who rattle through their fields and villages but seldom stop or leave anything behind but tire tracks and gasoline fumes.

More likely, I think, these women neither know nor care about such campaigns. Their lives move to deeper rhythms, rhythms that mystified and even offended the first colonial intruders from Europe, and now do the same to us, the latest intruders.

What are these rhythms? The closest I can come to identifying them is to call them gifts that these people give to everyone every day. Gifts of hospitality, concern, *presence.* Gifts that primarily spring from some source other than calculation.

At times, on other African assignments, I have tried to locate these rhythms within myself but could never do so. Soon enough I had abandoned the search and, reverting to the rhythms I did know, sunk back into my familiar spiritual lassitude, my numb soul dragging my sack of platitudes and pious certainties behind me.

As our truck approaches a small village we are greeted with enthusiastic waves and shouts from men and women, young and old, who idle on rough-hewn wooden chairs along the whitewashed mud walls of the narrow houses and shops that line the central square. The young men, struggling to stand out from their peers, wear knit wool hats or baseball caps with their visors off at an angle. Their objective is punk rakishness, but the effect is uninspired conformity.

The old-timers, far removed from fashion's fantasies, just look old.

The young women have a surer sense of themselves, with their bright frocks and elaborately cornrowed hair—mostly black hair, of course, but with a smattering of henna and occasionally even yellow and orange. I find their garish dyes oddly evocative, a bold reaching beyond the expected.

As we enter the town, the young people's enthusiasm bubbles to hilarity. Seemingly from nowhere, boys and girls ranging in age from six to sixteen materialize in the road and chase after us, laughing and shouting, straining to touch our outstretched hands. They wear T-shirts and shorts that flood the local markets from Asian sweatshops. None wear shoes. Their shirts sport pirated images of fading Western pop stars like Michael Jackson, Madonna, and the band Metallica, whose contorted faces, flaking off the shirts from countless washings, are silently frozen in midlyric hysteria.

The light shining from the children's faces diverts my attention from the tortured images on their shirts.

"Should we throw some coins to them?" I shout to our driver-guide over the whine of our truck's engine.

"No," he snaps at me over his shoulder, as if I thought our outing was a trip to the zoo.

"They don't want your money so much as to just touch you—make contact with you."

I think, "That's what I want, too."

Reza and I touch as many of their hands as we can reach.

The children run behind us for perhaps a quarter mile before dropping out, their excited shouts gradually fading away.

Silence returns.

I am euphoric.

Then the Clown—Kierkegaard's Clown—shows up again. He is sitting next to Reza on the bench across from me. He looks the same as always: floppy felt hat, bulbous red nose, flowery green shirt with big red polka dots, baggy brown suspendered trousers, outsized shoes with soles precariously detached.

"Hey, hotshot, have you figured it out yet?" he cries, jabbing his furled, lime green parasol in my direction, squirming in his seat, his stagy heartiness laced with mockery.

But his kohl-rimmed eyes are not mocking. They are pleading.

"Why *are* so many poor people in poor countries like this so happy—or if not quite happy, at least content? What's their secret? You must have some idea by now."

He doesn't pause for a reply. He knows I have none.

"You *have* figured *this* out though, haven't you, Paul ..." he says in a quieter tone, "... they know something you don't know, and you need to discover what it is, and start living as if you too believe it. And there isn't much time left, is there? The circus tent is still on fire, and if you don't get out soon, you'll die!"

I don't respond. In fact, I never respond directly to his question. I usually ponder it for a moment, but more likely than not, just as an answer begins to form in my mind, my thoughts will veer off onto other paths.

This is happening now.

My conscious mind is still savoring the delight of the children who had been so happy to chase after Reza and me. In fact, as I had watched them, the Clown's riddle had again vaguely occurred to me, like some half-forgotten monologue with myself—a monologue that I had told myself I had resolved but in reality a monologue that had crept back to me when I could no longer pretend that I had, in fact, resolved it.

Now that conversation has resumed. Again I see that haunting photograph from the Vietnam War: families streaming from their burning village, running from the American troops who, in panicked confusion, had just napalmed their huts. The image of a terrified girl of eight, her clothes burned off her body, running naked and screaming toward the cameraman, who might have taken the picture from the back of a truck just like the one that Reza and I—and the Clown—were riding in now.

The rich killing the poor. Is *this* what the Clown is warning me against?

My brutal reverie flees as quickly as it has come, and I refocus my thoughts on the laughing children who were chasing us.

The Clown is gone.

"Naturally," I think. He never hangs around long.

I glance toward Reza. He is gazing sleepily at the passing countryside, unaware that the Clown had even been there beside him.

I feel the familiar surge of dread.

Kierkegaard, a Dane, was a caustic and unorthodox Protestant philosopher who lived in the mid-nineteenth century and is seldom mentioned today without the taglines "Christian existentialist" and "leap of faith." He once told the story of a fire that broke out backstage at a circus and threatened to engulf the entire tent. To forestall panic, the manager sent out a clown to alert the audience to the danger and urge them to leave instantly.

But they thought the clown's increasingly frantic urgings were just his act—part of the show. They laughed, stayed put, and perished.

I think Kierkegaard's message is this: the world is a circus, and our salvation depends on our heeding those prophets who may look and sound like clowns but whose warnings about how we should live our lives—and tend to our salvation—we ignore at our own risk.

Of course, the trick has always been to distinguish the *real* clowns from the prophets like Kierkegaard's Clown. I always thought I could do this. Whenever Kierkegaard's Clown turned up as a priest, preacher, poet, or philosopher, I thought I could tell that he was not really a clown at all, but a prophet whose message was true. And when *other* kinds of clowns, wearing foolish costumes and spouting dire warnings, barged into my life's circus from time to time, I confidently ignored them.

Furthermore, I had always naively assumed that most other people were like me. I believed that they, too, knew that there was a reality deeper than the false "reality" proclaimed by the *real* clowns—the clowns who try to convince us that we can happily live on daily doses of amusement and diversion. I was convinced that while most people *seemed* to live their lives under the spell of this false "reality," deep down, like me, they knew what I knew: this false "reality" was mere illusion.

What *really* counted was whether our lives were in tune with the deeper reality, the reality that Kierkegaard's Clown kept badgering me about—a reality I could not see but, most of the time, could sense.

But lately I hadn't been so sure. Now, I think that most people actually believe that life's surface is the *only* reality. And, worse, I'm afraid that I might even be starting to agree with them. I'm afraid that I, too, have become so inured to life's constant infusions of false "reality" that I no longer know how to interpret *any* clown's message. In my indecision, I find myself becoming one of the circus audience who still listens to all the clowns but now ignores them all, refusing even to decide which are speaking truth and which are lying.

I just sit there, passively watching the clowns and the other performers—the jugglers, the freaks, the horses trotting in circles, the bears on bicycles, the elephants on balls, the lions on stools, snarling at their handlers—all of them trained to entertain me and tamp down the gnawing boredom and anxiety that now poison my spirit at every circus performance my spirit attends.

And, like a tiger that has snapped its chains, this morbid unease menacingly prowls the ground just outside the circus tent where I live my life.

I have returned to my room after having breakfast with Reza on the hotel terrace overlooking verdant, steamy gardens. Tiny brown birds with gold-flecked wings had brazenly darted about our table pecking at crumbs of toast and bits of fruit, hopping to within inches of us and defying us to do anything about it. The handfuls of other guests were sleekly dressed members of the local elite and desiccated, aging European couples—mostly Scandinavians—who seemed to be nursing hangovers.

I had not mentioned the Clown's appearance to Reza. I respected him and wanted his respect, and such a tale would certainly not have impressed him in any way that I would have wished.

Furthermore, I was still trying to take in just what had happened yesterday in the truck after Reza had dozed off, and the Clown had shown up. I think I know Reza well enough to suspect that he might share my puzzlement about the poor's ability to find contentment, but I'm not certain about it.

Raising a subject like the Clown with Reza would force him to focus on me and my quirks and not on the Clown.

I would wait.

I spend most of my life waiting.

But it seems that this time the Clown would not wait. I have flopped down on my unmade bed, already fatigued from the exertions of breakfast and small talk with Reza.

Then I notice him, perching on the chest of drawers opposite me.

"Surprised to see me again so soon?" he says, looking at me askance.

My pained expression answers for me.

"You know, Paul, you've been preaching your gospel to the poor of the world for years, trying to show them how the blessings of the American way of life, of living and working, can be transplanted in their countries if only they could be convinced to try them.

"But the more you try, the more confused you become, and the more you suspect that these people could teach *you* something.

"Am I right?"

I don't rise to his taunt. He doesn't seem to notice.

"Right here in The Gambia, you know that their way of farming, of growing food, makes more sense than all the tricks you have in your bag ... tricks about 'improved' strains of seeds.

"So here it's agriculture ... and in other places it's something else ... some other nostrum that promises the people prosperity but squashes the very thing they most value ... the thing you can't quite grasp ... the thing you call 'the secret of the poor.'"

I turn over in bed and lay facedown.

I don't need a lecture on how my career has been a big waste of time.

But the Clown is relentless.

"Face it, Paul, it's like pornography; you can't define it, but you know it when you see it. And you're coming to believe that *you* may be the pornographer. With your 'technical expertise' it is *you* who are introducing a dangerous and demoralizing stain into these people's lives, their culture—a stain that you and your colleagues label 'progress.'"

Now I'm angry.

"You know, friend ... you're a real jerk!

"Do you really think these people *want* to live poor? See their kids die young? Starve every few years? Die illiterate?"

The Clown looks away and lets loose a sigh.

"Of course not, Paul." His voice has lost its urgency.

"Relax ... you're doing *some* good!

"But you still ask yourself how these people live from day to day without hating their life and each other ... and without hating *you*, when your solutions fail them ... isn't *that* what's bugging you ... isn't *that* what you can't quite figure out about them?"

I don't respond.

"Let me try to help you," he says. "Let's go to the circus!"

Off to the Circus

*B*efore I can protest, the Clown has me by the wrist and is pulling me across a dusty field littered with trash and thick with weeds. Broken-down bicycles, metal folding chairs, and other detritus lay scattered about. Sheets of threadbare canvas tenting flap about in the stiff breeze like a beached flounder on the hot sand. A stray, yellowish cur warily lifts a hind leg against a spiky bush.

I am reminded of the grainy Italian movies I had seen as a teenager, usually starring Anna Magnani or Sofia Loren and directed by Antonioni, which I had not understood until many years later. I had wanted to see them again but could rarely find them in video rental shops.

Up ahead, in the distance, perhaps a hundred yards away, is a cluster of circus tents. Their canvas roofs sag to the ground from heights of perhaps forty feet, just barely supported by poles leaning at precarious angles.

As we draw closer I see that there are four tents in all. An unsmiling circus performer in tights comes into view from behind one of them, tottering on his rickety bicycle. A mustachioed roustabout with a mallet in his hands takes a halfhearted swing at a wooden tent stake whose frayed top resembles the bristles of a year-old toothbrush.

A faded and peeling billboard indicating the attraction inside marks each tent. The billboard in front of the nearest tent reads:

Tent No. 1: New York
Travel from Riches to Rags and Back in Two Hours!

The Clown lifts the flap and ushers me inside.

"Paul," he says, "if Americans knew how to fix poverty and improve people's lives, wouldn't you think they would do it here at home before trying to do it everywhere else?"

Immediately I find myself alone in a black tunnel. A familiar screeching roar surrounds me, and I realize that I am in a New York City subway. The Clown is beside me. I sit back in my plastic seat and wait.

The train rattles ever deeper into lower Manhattan, at each stop inhaling another surge of the tired and poor, most of them bound for the outer reaches of Brooklyn, past the East River and far beyond the close-in precincts of the rich, young, and oblivious. I know somehow that we had boarded the train in midtown, near the New York Public Library and had found the only vacant seats, but I am now standing, unable to ignore the hordes of poor, largely foreign born, New Yorkers who had boarded at later stops, clutching squirming infants and stuffed shopping bags from seedy discount stores.

We leave the train at Second Avenue, get our bearings, and head toward Maryhouse, the "hospitality house" for the poor on East Third Street.

Maryhouse is the home of the *Catholic Worker*, which is both the name of a newspaper published seven times a year ("a penny a copy") and a social justice movement. The newspaper has a worldwide readership exceeding eighty thousand, and the movement retains the prickly passion for the poor of its founder, Dorothy Day, who died in 1980.

I am jumpy. Although I have never been in the neighborhood before, I well remember the days, not so many years ago, when few strangers came anywhere near here without some pressing reason to do so.

Drunks and derelicts, men and women, mutter to themselves and the occasional passer-by. Homeless drifters slump on stairs and stoops. There is an odor of human decay and a pervasive sense of apprehensiveness.

The Clown is gone.

I see no nameplate on the hulking building's door. I push the buzzer but hear nothing and conclude that it is broken.

I glance up to the first row of windows, eight feet above street level. Each window is fitted with three horizontal bars, attached from the inside. Behind the bars I can see movement, and I shout up at it. Ten seconds later, the front door opens and an obviously distracted girl in her early twenties appears. She tells me that I can give to her any donation of food or clothing that I might have brought.

I explain that I have neither but would be happy to leave a small cash donation with her. Before she can respond I ask if I can take a few minutes to look around the mission and, perhaps, have a word with someone connected with the newspaper. I tell her that I would like to subscribe to it.

"Follow me," she says, softening, and leads me into a split foyer and up a broad flight of stairs to the main work area. From below I can hear the sounds of clattering dishes and smell a homey aroma wafting up from the dining room, where, I surmise, luncheon is being served to the mission's "clients."

My guide leads me to a small auditorium that takes up most of the space on the main floor. Long portable worktables have been crammed into the room, each bearing tall stacks of the *Worker*'s current edition. Several volunteers sit at the tables inserting the papers into mailing sleeves and sorting them by region.

Further into the room is a small raised stage, littered with furniture and props from past in-house theatrical productions. Along the far wall, stand mailbags, tagged by country—Albania through Zimbabwe. Other volunteers are stuffing the bags.

The parts of the walls that are visible behind the bags and bric-a-brac are plastered with fading posters and inspirational messages. A photograph of St. Thérèse of Lisieux as a young Carmelite nun stares out above the words, "I shall spend my Heaven doing good on Earth!" Nearby is a photo of a gaunt and frail Dorothy Day. And beneath the photo: "Don't call me a saint. I won't be dismissed so easily!"

My guide introduces me to Ted, who is supervising the volunteers, and, with a brisk farewell, leaves the room. Without any of the customary conversational preliminaries, Ted, an intense, balding wraith in his early forties, tells me how he had come to Maryhouse seven years ago after having worked with humanitarian projects in Appalachia and El Salvador.

He lives here, receives free room and board, and is in charge of getting the *Worker* wrapped, labeled, and mailed. Postage, the mission's biggest expense, comes from donations.

Ted says he's never been happier.

My memory flashes back to The Gambia—to the children chasing our pickup truck. Ted's happiness reminds me of the children's happiness—and my own happiness at having been there with them.

As we talk, other volunteers come and go. Ted introduces me to several of them (first names only), but none asks me about my work, family, or why I have come here.

Later I realize that I am just one of many weekly visitors who admire Dorothy Day's life and want to touch it in some way, however briefly.

I sign up to receive the *Catholic Worker* in the mail. I have a brief chat with its managing editor, a serene young matron who was raised in Los Angeles, and depart.

On the subway back uptown the Clown sits down next to me. I had not seen him get on.

No one else seems to see him at all, but I am used to that. These trips to the circus are always private, perhaps even imaginary.

He leans toward me and half whispers. "Dorothy Day said, 'Poverty is a mysterious thing. We need to be always writing and thinking about it. And, of course, striving for it.' Paul, you're *thinking* about it all right, but are you *striving* for it?"

I ignore his question. But my familiar self-conversation sputters back to life. I *don't* strive for poverty. I strive for comfort and respect. I strive for the kind of life that, in New York, is found north of Maryhouse. And as the train speeds me toward that happy land, the vaguely accusatory atmosphere of Maryhouse fades a bit more with every lurch.

At each stop the depressing poor are seamlessly supplanted by the focused strivers whose days and pockets are full, but whose vision is blurry.

But their clowns are on duty. They stare from every advertisement and croon into every iPod.

Soon enough all is as it should be. Winners up here, losers down there. The rich in their world, the poor in theirs.

In The Gambia, the trip between these two worlds requires a long and tiring flight. Here in New York, it takes just a few noisy subway stops.

I think I prefer the Gambian way and, thanks to Kierkegaard's Clown, *today* I'm choosing it.

I know I can always change my mind.

Tent No. 2: Moscow and Zagorsk
Mafia Capitalism Trumps Blazing Faith!

The taxi ride from Moscow to Zagorsk will take two hours, and my mood is foul. I can't even recall when the Clown dumped me in Moscow, but it was at least ten days ago.

I am interviewing bosses of American companies with operations in the new Russia. Our subject: the value of the many programs that Washington has devised to promote American investment in what until recently was the Soviet Union. Every man (no women lead these companies) has told me that he could not be doing business without the programs. The only problem is that the programs' financing is too small and grudging. They insist that unless it is vastly expanded and corporate eligibility requirements substantially lowered, an exodus of American companies will begin in two months, three at the most.

They have treated me to lavish vodka-soaked lunches at the handful of hideously expensive restaurants that have sprung up to serve them and their eager local acolytes.

On these occasions I have met these acolytes, the direct beneficiaries of Russia's suddenly atomized economy. Flanked by Armani-clad goons, weighed down by concealed weapons and encircled by luxuriously draped molls, these tyro tycoons—the *nomenklatura*—have eagerly adopted the standard *Godfather* mode of dress and attitude and brought it to a sinister boil that, were all this happening in America, would make Las Vegas seem like Mayberry.

At night, the good times roll on. Deafening discothèques, their twirling strobe lights singling out dancers in dark corners like escapees from the gulag, rage till dawn. The Americans and their Russian companions, conjoined in an officially sanctioned and unregulated gold rush, are having too much fun to ever let it end. And they expect me to play my part by reporting their requirements to Washington precisely as they have transmitted them to me.

But I'm not so sure.

Whenever I finally manage to extricate myself from the satanic turmoil, usually by pleading an early morning appointment, I have to walk down the Arbat, where scores of Moscow's old, exhausted, and forgotten line both sides of the street, selling worn-out kitchen utensils, tattered clothing, and, most heartbreakingly, treasured personal items like wedding rings and silver.

No matter how late the hour or icy the March wind, I always stop and inspect some of the items, more as if to signal that I can understand their desperation and pain than to actually buy anything.

But, as usual, I also have a selfish motive: I want to know how they do it. I want to know how this woman has reached old age with no security whatsoever, or how that haunting young woman with pale green eyes and high, spectral cheekbones, trying to scrounge kopeks for food, keeps herself and her infant alive.

I never learn the answer. When I disengage and walk away empty-handed, they invariably bless me and wish me well, passing silently over the cosmic unfairness that made me the secure voyeur from a distant fairy-land and them the poverty-blasted circus-goers mired in this dead world.

Perhaps I should invite the Arbat ladies to a discothèque.

It is Sunday now, and I want to get out of Moscow for some air. I have settled on Zagorsk, a rural neighborhood of Orthodox churches and monasteries that, I have been told, recalls an older Russia—a prerevolutionary Russia whose remnants barely survive.

Will the prosperity that I am in Russia to promote show any green shoots in Zagorsk? Even before getting there, I know the answer.

The taxi hurtles over decaying roads through the blighted countryside. Winter is waning, but lethal shards of rock-hard ice are still sunk into the stubbled fields that stretch through the gelid air to the horizon. From time to time a peasant, usually an old, stooped, and scarf-swathed woman, can be seen in the distance poking in the frozen ground foraging for a potato or some other edible root.

Zagorsk itself bustles with activity. There is a large square in the middle of the village. Four small churches face the square, their familiar onion domes painted in gay colors that even in the wan spring light cast a hopeful glow.

A horse-drawn troika circles around the square, pulling a sled filled with delighted children whose chain-smoking parents watch from the small bandstand in the center.

I ask my driver to wait for me and walk across the square to the nearest church. As I draw near I can smell incense. Then I see its thin wisps seeping from the shuttered stained glass windows along the side of the church. From inside I hear the muffled strains of soaring Russian hymns.

The entrance to the church is packed tight, and I have to push and squirm my way past some older persons to even get a glimpse of the altar. Old men, their frayed jackets sagging away from their bodies under the weight of tarnished military medals, stand among old women, many of whom clutch lighted two-foot-long candles as they weep and sing out.

I stand there for at least forty-five minutes, lost in the hymns' thrilling harmonies. I wonder how these people, inured as they are to modernity's harshest lashes, muster the faith to yet again call on God to help them in this, their latest role, the disintegrating chrysalis of Russia's latest metamorphosis.

In the taxi ride back to Moscow, the Clown shows up again. The driver gives no indication that he notices him.

"Christ, it's cold!" the Clown hisses.

"Paul, is it easier to be poor in a warm climate? I think so, at least on the surface of life. Fewer clothes ... easier to grow food ... at least you won't freeze to death! ... But then, Russia may be the exception. Even if it were in the tropics, there's something about the despair and cynicism here that goes beyond poverty.

"Sure, they're poor ... desperately poor ... but their problems go much deeper than that. You got anything in your bag for them?"

His voice trails off. Then, shuddering like a horse twitching flies from its flanks, he withdraws to his stall of rue and keeps silent for the rest of the trip back to Moscow.

Tent No. 3: Luang Prabang
A Buddhist Cave, Bugs for Lunch, The Poor Give Alms!

We make our way warily from the recessed top of the cave back down to the "cigarette boat" that has been tied up at the rickety pier at the cave's entrance, a hundred feet below on the south bank of the Mekong River. It has been an arduous trek up the limestone steps that snake in a switchback pattern upward and deeper into the cave's dank recesses.

The Clown lags behind the group. Of course, only I know he's there.

As we climb, we pass hundreds of primitively carved statues of the Buddha, ranging in size from three inches to six feet. They are grouped together in scores of small altars most of which have been hewn from the limestone floor and walls.

Interspersed among the statues are votive candles, jammed randomly into the altars' crevices. Many are burned to a nub; others gutter in the stifling gloom, giving off only the dimmest glow. Bats, suspended from the ceiling, rustle and squeak as we pass beneath them, but otherwise they ignore us.

The cigarette boat tips unsettlingly as our group of ten tourists gingerly climbs aboard. Our guide fires up the raucous outboard motor, and we head downstream, angling toward the north bank of the river.

Ten minutes later we are there. Our guide cuts the engine, and we drift the last forty feet to the shore.

Then they are here. Dozens of people from the village that is just out of sight beyond a rise, shuffle down to the bank to greet us.

The men, emaciated and wiry, hang back in watchful embarrassment, constantly refolding their brightly colored sarongs around their waists. They wear no other clothing.

The women and children throng near the spot where our boat has been pulled up on the bank. They launch into a spirited competition for our attention. "Crafts" and jewelry appear from the ubiquitous woven plastic fiber sacks that I always call "Asia bags." The high-pitched shouts and frantic gestures alarm me at first, but it is the show that follows that grips me.

An ancient and wrinkled crone, cradling a woven basketful of wriggling brown crickets, drops to a squat in front of us. Making sure she has our full attention, she scoops a handful into her mouth, crunches them to paste with her few remaining teeth, and swallows.

After smacking her lips in a show of satisfaction, she repeats the performance twice, all the while checking our reaction, knowing from long practice that it will be one of fascinated disgust.

Several of us drop a few notes of the almost worthless local currency, the kip, into her hand and try to disengage to walk to the village behind the rise. But she won't permit it.

Still holding her basket of crickets, now almost empty, she herds us single file to her hut at the edge of the village and indicates that we should wait for a minute. She ducks into the hut and in seconds emerges with several short strands of white cotton string draped over her left arm.

Our guide, off to the side, indicates that we should extend our left arms and let the woman tie one of the strings around our left wrists. He repeats over and over the word *baci,* which we later learn is the name of this intimate Lao ceremony that marks the arrivals and departures of friends.

As we are saying farewell to our hostess, we hear in the distance the soft sound of tinkling bells and the rhythmic beating of a small drum. Presently, a line of Buddhist monks, perhaps twelve in all, approaches us on an overgrown footpath. They range in age from the young, perhaps fifteen years of age, to the quite old, perhaps eighty. Most of them seem to be in their late twenties to midforties. Their heads are shaved, and all wear saffron robes—on one end of which they sling over one shoulder, leaving the other shoulder bare. They are barefoot. Each carries a small brass begging bowl and keeps his eyes lowered.

As they approach us, our hostess abruptly switches her attention from us to them. She quickly ducks back into her hut and, in seconds, reemerges with a small basket of the glutinous "sticky" rice, a food much favored by the Lao. Facing the footpath, she drops to her knees and sits back on her heels. Several other village women appear and take up positions on either side of our hostess. Most of them also hold small rice baskets; two or three hold baskets of vegetables and two others hold baskets of kip.

The monks file slowly past the kneeling women, who scoop offerings into the monks' bowls. In this moment of ritual communion, our party has been completely forgotten. Poor beggars and even poorer alms-givers play stylized roles dating from the Buddha's time on earth. No further thoughts of prying a few kip from the tourists. An ancient rhythm takes over. The poor succor the poor.

Some of us in awkward embarrassment begin to fish some kip from our pockets to give the monks. But they are already moving again, toward the next village. We have no further role to play here.

Forty-five minutes later, the Clown and I are back in our boat and heading toward our tour bus in Luang Prabang.

Tent No. 4: Phnom Penh
The Army Museum Has Skulls & Bones—and Glory!

The monsoon lashes the plate-glass windows of the neighborhood restaurant where four Nigerian soldiers in combat fatigues slouch over giant bottles of beer, staring at a small television set showing a Thai soap opera. They are part of the UN peacekeeping force, but things are quiet, and they are bored—dusky centurions confusingly adrift in this soft Asian setting.

I have been in Phnom Penh for five days conducting a legal training program and have been cooped up in desultory classes in which I have been lecturing Cambodian legal officials, most of whom are in their twenties, on the finer points of legislative drafting.

I know that, at best, they are taking in far less than half of what I am telling them, but that doesn't concern me. Learning is a long-term process, and I will be long gone before that process is even partly understood here.

Today is Saturday, and there are no classes scheduled until Monday. I am staying in a nearby guesthouse and have gone to the restaurant for lunch—a familiar bowl of soup and beef on a stick. It is spicy and filling, and after lunch, the fearsome gale makes me abandon any thought of looking around town. I join the Nigerians for beer.

A visiting Vietnamese businessman, alone at an adjoining table, earnestly tries to engage me in conversation. He assures me that his English is "first rate," but I can barely understand him. Meanwhile, my Nigerian friends are speaking rapidly in their own version of English—a singsongy mélange of a patois and uncertainly assimilated Briticisms—that make them as incomprehensible to me as the Vietnamese fellow.

In short, we English-speakers need an interpreter.

After an hour of this earnest but incoherent fellowship, I have had enough. I announce that, notwithstanding the foul weather, which has by now swamped the street outside in a foot of water and shows no signs of subsiding, I am going to tour the Army Museum. It is about a mile away, but I know its visiting hours and know that getting there, even in this weather, will be more interesting than staying here at the restaurant.

I peer out the window and through the downpour see several cyclo drivers sheltering under an awning across the street. They are leaning on their cyclos, which are bolted to canvas-covered one-person cabs in front. They have removed their sandals and rolled their trousers to their knees. I do the same and, opening the door, slosh across the street and climb into the lead cyclo.

The startled driver peers over my shoulder as I point out the museum on my tattered tourist map. He then mounts his cyclo and laboriously pedals into the tempest, pushing me forward in the fully enclosed cab.

After ten minutes he can go no further through the water. He dismounts and pushes the cyclo to the curb. Then he unfurls a tattered umbrella, quite useless in the deluge, and motions to me to dismount and duck under it as he guides me to a shuttered shop-house twenty feet away. We slide into a narrow alley next to the shop on the ground floor, and he indicates that I should follow him up a flight of slippery wooden stairs attached to the outside of the building, to the living quarters above.

I am reluctant to comply, but his request is so urgent that I do so. He pushes open the door at the top of the steps and I follow him inside, glad to be out of the storm.

Huddled inside is a family—husband and wife in their early thirties, three children ranging in age from six months to three years, and four old-timers, doubtless the grandparents. The small television set is on, but no one is watching it. Plates of half-eaten food lie about on low tables.

My driver speaks quickly to the family in Khmer, now hushed and staring at me, obviously explaining our sudden visit. Then, turning to me and using hand signals, he indicates that we will linger here until the rain eases.

Then all reserve melts, and the young parents, in tortured English, press food and drink on me, ignoring my attempts to tell them that I have just had lunch. The two older children shyly approach me and, at the apparent urging of their parents and grandparents, begin jerkily turning in imitation of the slow, stylized manner of Khmer dance. They are entertaining me. Their elders look on in rapt approval. I politely applaud their performance.

One of the grandmothers offers me the couch to stretch out on, vacating it for a small stool nearby. After a pro forma protest, I accept, and soon my eyes are closed and the drumming of the rain on the roof lulls me toward sleep. The children keep dancing; I can hear their shuffling feet. They make no other sound.

Suddenly I awake. The rain has stopped, and the silence has disturbed my fitful nap. I check my watch. I have been asleep just under an hour. The adults are gone, but the children are still here, slumped together in the corner of the room, staring at me as if in reproach for my nodding off during their dance.

The cyclo driver reappears and silently motions me to my feet. The others are nowhere to be seen. Outside I see that the sun is high. The humidity is almost toxic, and as I climb into the cyclo's cab, I am enfolded in a damp and gauzy mist.

After a ten-minute ride through streets still flooded with a foot of water, we stop in front of the ticket office of the Army Museum. I confirm that that the museum is open and try to pay and dismiss my driver. He waves me off, making me understand that he will wait for me to finish my visit and then return me to my hotel, or wherever else I might wish to go.

Once inside the main door I soon realize that I am the only visitor. A woman approaches me from the cloakroom. She appears to be in her early forties, but her dull eyes and diffident manner make her age difficult to estimate. She walks in a lethargic way that at once makes me think how ridiculous it is that this country, this capital city, that needs so much just to survive, thinks it necessary to support a museum dedicated to Cambodia's military disasters falsely depicted as glorious victories.

My guide wears what appears to be a uniform. The nametag says Tisa, and beneath the name is a tiny Union Jack, indicating, I hope, that she can speak English. She slowly looks me over and then speaks.

"Would you like a tour?" Just the hint of a sly smirk, I think. Her English is good.

"Yes, I would."

She leads me to the first hall, which is devoted to molding depictions of battles from the French colonial period.

Then Kierkegaard's Clown sidles up to me. I knew my luck couldn't last.

"Are you really going to leave it to this miserable creature to explain the historical significance of this place? You know she can barely speak English and will only be parroting the Party line!

"You need my help! I'm going to tag along behind you both, and make sure get the *real* story this place is telling."

Tisa begins her well-rehearsed but barely audible and largely incomprehensible spiel.

Then, close behind me, the Clown's shadow tour begins in the World War I hall. As if declaiming a Horatian ode, he portentously starts in. Only I can hear him.

> *Walls in hues of sundried blood*
> *suck in the numbing heat and light—*
> *within these walls, stone-sealed and sere,*
> *a crypt for Buddha's people here—*
> *echo the screams that froze the night.*
>
> *Surrounding lawn, unkempt and blotched,*
> *now like the fields of upland rice—*
> *deserted like those very fields—*
> *mine-strewn paddies that no rice yields.*
> *One might cross once, but seldom twice.*
>
> *The lone guide, Tisa, turns the key*
> *and leads him to a musty lair*
> *where Kampuchea's battles roar—*
> *Christ! Have they always been at war!—*
> *in dioramas of despair.*
>
> *She starts with France—cool French élan—*
> *the Galois smoke, the Gallic flair—*
> *'We're here to bring you lasting peace …*
> *vraiment mission civilatrice!'*
> *The haughty toss of head, the stare …*
>
> *that calmed French nerves in the Great War—*

Picardy, Ypres, the Marne, the Somme—
all youth was lost, a nation quailed,
Marianne cried … but evil failed.
Here, evil wins, and colons come

to sink the tricolor in soil
where rice once grew to feed these few
whose ageless rhythms throbbed unseen
by those who called this 'Indochine,'
this place that Malraux thought he knew.

(Malraux the thief—he knew just how
rare Ankhor icons could inflate
his fame in France. This would assure
for him, alors, Legion d'Honneur—
O happy turn for this man's fate!)

Tisa leads me out of the World War I gallery and into the World War II gallery. The Clown was right. She barely seems to know what we're looking at through the scratched and dusty display cases.

Among the faded photographs on the walls, Pol Pot makes his first appearance, a jaunty jungle buccaneer. A photo shows the Asian Che Guevara holed up in the bush with his comrades, waiting for the right time to strike.

But Tisa doesn't mention his name. Probably still afraid to, I think.

But, never mind. Right on cue, the Clown provides the historical context.

Strong France again, in World War II,
when stern de Gaulle, in London, kept
the flame and scorned defeatist mood.
But Petain, calling evil good,
let Free France fall as all France wept.

And further back, O Citoyens!
when Rights of Man spawned Rule of Mob,
no room for any humane thought
in one more hell that Reason wrought—
despair for toutes Les Miserables!

Esprit struck down as Reason reigned,
elixir for unanchored minds …
but once again, as unease grew,
malignant terror bloomed anew,
and, once again, France drew the blinds.

And, in our time, sane voice of France—
Pascal, Bergson—even Descartes—
none like them was there to warn
of this new terror, theory-born.
All France fell silent—all but Sartre.

Sartre—philosophe for modern man
(for modern woman, his Simone)—
who bullied dimmer intellects
with sophistries and, one suspects,
laughed softly when he was alone.

Shamed by dark secrets from a war
which bald evasions could not hide,
some sought in Sartre the means to quell
the premonition of a hell
of guilt that welled from deep inside.

While most scorned Sartre's despairing themes,
a rootless few believed the lot,

and one of them, of credulous sort,
slouched straight toward him from Calais port:
the Kampuchean called Pol Pot.

Then Tisa and I move to the exhibits dating from the mid-1970s, when the illegal and secret American bombing of Cambodia began in earnest, as the American people were turning decisively against the war in Vietnam. The bombs dislodged the country's civilization, and Pol Pot, "Brother Number One," sprang from his jungle redoubt and shoveled his people into a very special hell.

Plastic cabinets chock full of human skulls stand side by side against the far wall like sentries at attention.

There are photographs showing hopeless refugees tramping along the dusty roads leading to the mountains and, almost certainly, to death from overwork and starvation.

Tisa again seems oddly detached from her surroundings. Or, I think, has her spirit succumbed to the banality of evil—the only way to keep one's sanity in the daily presence of this homegrown Armageddon?

The Clown is not at a loss for words.

The hall that's next on Tisa's tour
depicts what Sartrean gospel yields
when gulped down whole by rootless men
who will not see the Seine again,
but make their own Champs: killing fields.

Scenes of horror, bone, and blood,
stark skulls which bear brute savage strikes,
and, close at hand, a cabinet
in which the skulls are neatly set,
like Bastille's heads atop their pikes.

Those skulls, bleached white—and each is cleft
by blades that struck above the ear.
(For such mass murder why waste lead

when axes make sure all are dead?)
Pol-Potted holocaust lies here!

And did he dream of France—perhaps
a smart café where Sartre's shade mulls?
Or, Brother Number One might yawn
and dream he's on the Sun King's lawn,
playing at boules with Khmer skulls.

The tour is over. Tisa conducts me toward the entrance, her attitude noticeably lightening with each step away from the hall of horrors.
The all-seeing Clown is ready.

The tour is done, and out they go
where faded tanks in ranks all neat
flank mold-damp MiGs to rust away
beneath tin roofs which seem to sway,
battered by the day's white heat.

But just before they move outside
Tisa takes his hand in hers
and lewdly looks into his eyes.
He, barely hiding his surprise,
is startled, and at once demurs.

She then begins to pluck his shirt
from where sweat plasters it to skin
and lets her eyes, in mute entreat,
bid him recline on a soft seat
with her, in a dim room within.

Now we are just outside the main entrance. After an awkward few moments in which I only gradually understand Tisa's muttered suggestion, I hastily tip her and hurry out to the curb and to my waiting driver, who climbs onto his cyclo.

As I approach him, I catch a glimpse of the Clown from the corner of my eye. I know the driver cannot see him.

The Clown catches up to me about fifty yards from the cyclo.

"I have a final stanza for you, Paul! I wrote it down. Here, take it!

"It sums up your thoughts, especially about the French. I must say, I'm mystified by your conviction that they are actually nobler than they act most of the time."

I shrug but do not respond.

He places a crumpled sheet of paper in my left hand. I glance down at it and try to read his scrawled writing.

"Read it later, friend," he said.

Then he is gone.

The cyclo returns me to my hotel alongside the river that runs through the city. I flop exhausted on my bed, fish the Clown's final stanza from my pocket, and read it.

> *Enameled nails, all-knowing smile,*
> *a night scene from Bois de Boulogne,*
> *he barely hears the murmured cost:*
> *two dollars. What's there to be lost?*
> *He hesitates. She leads him on.*
>
> *He pauses—then he moves away.*
> *She catches him at the front door*
> *and bids him sign the guestbook there.*
> *He writes: "Cambodia, from where*
> *I stand, you must for evermore*
>
> *forswear 'solutions' like the ones*
> *with which Pol Pot and sour Sartre*
> *wrought havoc on your lovely land,*
> *Sartre blindly guiding Pol Pot's hand.*
> *Be Kampuchea—that's your part!*

Forswear what fueled those hate-wracked days
when genocide became the norm,
when you were wed to woe for years
by theories which ignored your tears.
Take refuge now from that cruel storm.

And, France … what can one say to you,
whose sins and sons still haunt this land
where once you ruled but now retreat,
cowering in full defeat,
to vainly wash your bloodstained hand?

Reclaim the role that God intends,
a beacon for both good and grace.
Your struggle for gloire is vain
as long as you inflict the pain
that keeps you from a saner place …

a place of beauty, calm, and light,
a place where art and spirit thrive,
a place where all may come to see
what God waits yet for you to be:
a place where Man can be alive!"

I quickly read the stanza, and then read it again, more slowly. Then I fold the paper and put it back in my pocket. I mutter to myself: Dante had Virgil to guide him through hell. My guide through Cambodia's hell—my Virgil—is a clown.

Port Tobacco

Port Tobacco is a sleepy little town in eastern Maryland that in colonial days was a bustling trading hub. Today, if it's known for anything at all, it's for being the site of the first Carmelite convent in the United States, dating from 1790. Its population has shrunk to a handful of people, many of whom are professionals who set their own schedules, working for government agencies and private organizations based in Washington, forty miles away.

I am one of those people. Although Port Tobacco is well within the reach of Washington's newspapers, television signals, and tedious self-importance (which I never confuse with self-awareness), I like its rural feel and convenience to my consulting company employers.

I have been back home for almost two weeks and, as usual after returning from an assignment, I am exhausted.

Frank Stefano is perhaps the last person I want to hear from. Could I drop by his office later in the day? He has a visitor he wants me to meet. "Who is it?" I ask, but he puts me off. His evasiveness annoys me.

"Paul! Come in!" he exclaims when I appear outside his door two hours later. He leaps from his chair, rushes toward me, all orchestrated affability and moist palm as he shepherds me into his office. He asks about my trip to The Gambia, distractedly ignores my response, and introduces me to his visitor, Father Geli, a rail-thin, gray-haired priest of medium height and a stern demeanor intensified by his trim black cassock.

I recognize him immediately. I had seen that face before—a seamless combination of self-conscious piety and ecclesiastical hauteur—thoroughly French. But I can't immediately place him.

Then, when he greets me in French, I remember. We had met some fourteen months ago, here in Port Tobacco. Some of the mortal remains of St. Thérèse of Lisieux had arrived at the convent just down the road, and Father Geli, together with another French priest, whose name I had also forgotten, had been with them.

Starting in 1997, the relics had toured the world to commemorate the hundredth anniversary of the saint's death at the age of twenty-four from tuberculosis in her Carmelite convent in Normandy. The tour was to have taken a year, but popular demand had extended it to four years, and even now no end is in sight.

Millions of Thérèse's devotees had clamored to see the relics of this cloistered nun whose autobiography—written at the insistence of the convent's aristocratic abbess—expresses an apparently naïve but actually complex spirituality that had propelled her quickly to sainthood.

Port Tobacco had been the first stop of the U.S. segment of the world tour, and it had fallen to Frank Stefano, as the town's part-time mayor, to play official host to the hundreds of pilgrims and clergy who would crowd into town to venerate the relics. I was the town's only French-speaker whom Frank knew, and when he had asked me to chair the relics' welcoming committee, I could not refuse.

At the time I had known little about Thérèse. I remembered seeing her photo on the wall at Maryhouse in New York and knew that she was known as the "Little Flower," but that saccharine sobriquet had effectively drained away any curiosity about her that I might originally have harbored, and I had relegated her to the legions of plaster saints venerated by pious old women and young women who were themselves, in an earlier time, most likely bound for convents.

In fact, I am not the "Little Flower" type at all. My French literary favorites are a decidedly secular, even decadent crowd, ornaments of a culture that surely would have scandalized Thérèse and her parents: Rimbaud, Proust, Flaubert, Baudelaire, and Camus. In a perverse sort of way, I have even been exploring Houellebecq. Not exactly the Christian branch of French literature.

After some brief banter among the three of us, Father Geli takes command. Thérèse's relics are scheduled to leave the States for their next stop, in Latin America, but Father's superior, a French bishop, had called him yesterday with a change of itinerary.

He had told Father Geli that a week ago the Latin-rite archbishop of Iraq, himself a Carmelite, had sent the bishop an urgent request that the relics go next to Baghdad and a handful of other Iraqi cities so that Thérèse's many Christian and Muslim devotees might more easily focus their prayers for her intercession. They wanted to stop what appeared to be the imminent American bombing and full-scale invasion that would inevitably follow.

The American government said it was convinced that the terrorists who had reportedly flown planes into buildings in New York and Washington almost eighteen months ago had had connections to Saddam Hussein and his brutal regime. The Americans wanted to conquer and occupy Iraq now. The European Union, the United Nations, and the pope were trying in vain to convince them to delay such a drastic step, and let diplomacy proceed. Franco-American relationships in particular were seriously frayed.

Father Geli says that the bishop had consented to sending the relics to Iraq for three weeks, from Saturday, March 1, to Friday, March 21. Then Father Geli comes to the point.

Two days ago, his colleague, who had been assisting him on the North American leg of the tour, had been questioned by U.S. immigration authorities regarding some remarks he had made in a television interview about the change in the tour's itinerary. The immigration officials had thought his tart remarks insufficiently pro-invasion. They had seized his passport, and there was no assurance that the matter would be resolved in time for him to accompany Father Geli and the relics to Iraq. Departure was in just nine days.

Yesterday Father Geli had asked Frank Stephano's advice about the matter, and Frank had suggested that I fill in for the detained colleague. Frank had stressed that I was Catholic, spoke French, had worked in the Middle East, and that Father Geli and I had previously met. In short, Frank told Father Geli that I would be perfect for the task.

Father Geli instantly agreed.

"You will be replaced by someone within three weeks after we get there—either by my detained colleague or someone else from France," Father Geli says with an offhand shrug. But there is something else in his voice—something that seems intended to convey to me that my demurral would be at the very least selfish and possibly even cowardly—a craven rejection of potential martyrdom, perhaps.

"Will you do it, Paul?" he asks, using the familiar form of address that in any other circumstances would have been inconceivable for a Frenchman addressing someone he had met only once before. "Will you go with me to Iraq with Thérèse's reliquary? We will take care of all your expenses, of course."

I try to grasp the implications of Father Geli's narrative. What if the American bombing begins when we are in Baghdad and traps us there for the duration of the war? Even now, how safe is it for Americans in Iraq just before a probable invasion? Western companies and aid organizations are already pulling staff out of the country in anticipation of war.

Playing for time, I mention my concerns, adding that I am flattered to have been asked.

Father Geli has obviously anticipated my concerns.

"The Americans would not risk harming the relics," he sniffs. "Think of the uproar among Catholic voters here in this country. Your government doesn't want that. We'll be perfectly safe."

Not altogether convincingly, he resumes his efforts to minimize the risks and concludes with what he obviously thinks is the clincher.

"And don't forget," he had says, lowering his tone to a reverential whisper, "we'll be protected by St. Thérèse herself, who will certainly keep us safe."

Checkmate.

I am not devout enough to place much hope in saintly protection, but I keep the thought to myself. I say I will think it over and call Frank with my decision the next morning. If I decline, Father Geli will still have a few days to find someone else.

I didn't think it over. I knew from the start that I would do it. I had nothing to hold me back. My parents were deceased and a year ago. Jenny had finally packed up and left me—tired of being in a relationship that she had at length decided was bound neither for her idea of marriage nor much else that she wanted in life. I was a no-longer-young "democracy expert" whose only real constituent had voted with her feet. In a fit of my habitual, long-perfected knack for denial, I had done what had been perfectly predictable: I had tried to "put all that behind me" and fill my life with yet more work and travel, knowing full well that that wouldn't heal my hurt at having failed to face the reasons for my empty life, or at least discover what the reasons were. But I really hadn't known what else to do. I would call Frank tomorrow, but now I just wanted a drink—maybe a few drinks—and went home to get started.

The phone won't stop ringing, and I finally pick it up. I had passed out on the couch, and my head is throbbing. It is ten o'clock at night.

Reza Krishen is on the line, from his home in India.

I force myself to focus and to sound coherent, but doubt that I am fooling him. I think he must have sensed my real attitude of sullen annoyance. I had long ago e-mailed the draft of my Gambia "deliverable" to him, incorporated most of his return comments into my draft, and submitted the final document to Talbot ("Shadow") Peirce, our supervisor in Washington. I have never actually met Peirce and do not want to hear now from Reza that I need to do more work on it before getting paid.

Reza does not mention The Gambia or the "deliverable."

"I hear you're going to take a trip, Paul. I was talking to Shadow Peirce, and he told me. He didn't tell me how he knew your plans."

I feel a chill. My first thought is that either Frank Stefano or Father Geli has told USAID that they had asked me to go to Iraq and have sought the agency's support in convincing me to do so. But I know almost immediately that that is ridiculous. What is not ridiculous is that my conversation with Frank and Father Geli had been recorded and its substance given to Peirce. Now Peirce is using Reza to ask me for a favor. I am certain of it.

As if to avoid hearing my angry reaction, Reza keeps talking.

"Shadow wants you to do a favor for him over there. You'll be paid, of course—and at a far more generous rate than you and I are used to. But he wants to meet you before you go. Can you do that tomorrow … in DC … you know, just to get acquainted?"

Reza hasn't paused, not even to take a breath. Clearly he has carefully rehearsed his script and is anxious to get through it.

I don't know whether to feel afraid or reassured. I don't like being spied upon; yet, in truth, it doesn't really surprise me. I tell myself that having someone like Peirce and his hidden handlers—obviously CIA—know that I am in Iraq might even give me another layer of security there. But, in fact, I know that any connection to Peirce and his friends, no matter how flimsy, could make my visit more dangerous, not less so.

After enduring a few perfunctory remarks from me, Reza seems anxious to end the conversation. He is doubtless using a scrambled line but still does not want to give me any time to quiz him. He quickly wishes me well and says good-bye.

Impulsively, I call Frank at home, consciously pleased to have wakened him. I tell him that I will go to Iraq with Father Geli and the relics. Frank mumbles congratulations on my "brave and selfless" decision. I reply that I am sure there is nothing to worry about.

Of course, I don't believe it.

Peirce is just over six feet tall and looks to be in his early fifties. He has the build of a fullback and the unmistakable whiff of the best men's club in Washington. I am sure he plays a mean game of squash. His thinning hair is sandy, and his pale blue eyes, somewhat bloodshot, are steady. Only the roseate web of broken spider veins on his cheeks suggest that his relentlessly bluff manner might owe something to drink. His charcoal gray trousers are held up by a hemp belt, adding a louche but clearly calculated touch of clubby yet earnest endeavor.

"Thanks for coming into town, Paul. You and I should have met long ago!

"Have a chair."

The office is large and airy. Peirce is selling something and wants to get the atmospherics right. We take seats at a small coffee table, and he starts his pitch.

"I'm the guy they're sending to Iraq to make sure the invasion doesn't get blindsided by some unforeseen off-the-wall surprise ... something that perhaps we should have seen coming but didn't ... something that fell through the cracks, you could say.

"What really has the Pentagon's knickers in a twist is the fear that we might lose the moral high ground—that we are seen, for example, as a bully just interested in grabbing Iraq's oil and building bases, and not really interested in getting rid of Saddam's weapons of mass destruction and giving the people a shot at democracy—the good life."

It is hard to take Peirce seriously—but it is clear that he himself is deadly serious. I put on a solemn face and hope I can sustain it.

Peirce plows ahead.

"The guys are particularly concerned that this 'clash of civilizations' garbage doesn't become boiled down in the public's mind as the godless West bullying the God-fearing East. That's the kind of psyops battle we could lose, big time. That's why we tried to get the pope to sign off on the war—you know, let us brand it as 'just.'

"You may know he didn't go for that, and we half expected that he wouldn't—but we hardly expected him to come up with his own idea—some cockamamie scheme called the Akbar Club!"

He takes a sip of his Diet Coke—I had declined one—and moves on.

"As I understand it, he's identified a group of local navel-gazers from various religions who he hopes will try to get people in Iraq to find common religious ground. He wants the chances for religious and ethnic violence kept at a minimum. Some kind of 'Kumbaya' can't-we-all-just-get-along thing."

"That really blew us away!"

It is getting harder for me to keep a straight face.

"So we *had* to play along—we figured, if we didn't, he might go public—say we refused to try it. Our Catholic base might not like that. And the whole goddamn thing was dropped in *my* lap, for chrissake!"

I feel as if I am sliding into a twilight zone. I haven't said much yet, and so far I don't feel I need to.

Peirce shows no sign of slowing down.

"I didn't have the foggiest notion of how to proceed with this Akbar Club thing. Then I saw a small piece in the *Post* about St. Thérèse's relics leaving the States for Iraq. I called the mayor of the town in Maryland where the relics were then located—Frank something. His name had been in the article. I told him I was about to go to Baghdad, too, and that if there was any way I could help with the relics, let me know. I figured some association with those bones might give me some leverage with that nutty club.

"Frank told me that he was trying to convince you to go there with the relics. I thought, 'This is my lucky day!' I recognized your name from several USAID projects, but I didn't recall ever having actually met you. So I called our old friend Reza in India to see if you were the same guy I thought you were. Reza confirmed that you were, and it was then that I asked him to call you—and you know the rest.

"Small world, huh!"

Peirce and I are now joined in the room by five men. Peirce goes through the motions of introducing them to me, using first names only. One of them announces that the slide show has been set up in the conference room and, "We're ready to go."

I'm still utterly in the dark.

We all troop inside to a small conference room and seat ourselves around a table, facing a screen that has been set up next to a nearby wall.

Peirce starts a laptop that projects the title page of the presentation onto the screen:

The Akbar Club: Spiritual Support for Implementing Democracy Under Fire

Then one of the newcomers says, "OK, guys, you know the drill."

Peirce shoots me an embarrassed glance, trying to distance himself from what was coming next. Everyone around the table joins hands—my two neighbors take mine—and bows his head. Then, in unison:

If a sparrow cannot fall without His knowledge,
Can an Empire rise without His help?

Peirce then runs through some slides that reprise much of his earlier conversation about the "just war" argument that the pope had rejected. They show photographs of three conservative American scholars and theologians alongside some of their better-known quotations supporting the notion that war on Iraq is "just."

There is no slide showing the pope's response.

The next series of slides is labeled "Pax Americana." Is the use of Latin an appropriation of a bit of the Catholic Church's heritage as a peevish riposte to the pope? The final slides begin with a brief overview of the government's plans to "extend its reach" throughout the world. Then they show a brightly colored map of Central Asia—from Turkey and Azerbaijan in the west, extending eastward across the Caspian Sea to Turkmenistan, Kazakhstan, Uzbekistan, Afghanistan, Tajikistan, Kyrgyzstan, and ending at the western border of China.

"This," intones Peirce, "is the 'Great Game'—what it's all about."

"This is the prize," he says. "After Saudi and Iraq and Iran go dry, these dudes will have the rest of the world's oil and gas, and if we don't grab it now, the Russians, Indians, and Chinese will. If we get there first we'll be set for the next two hundred years at a minimum.

"The only problem is, these guys are Muslims—even the Chinese in this region are Muslims. They got some other religions going on, too, but they're overwhelmingly hajjis. And we need to use everything in our bag to get 'er done—military force, religion, whatever it takes to 'win their hearts and minds.'"

"And their oil!" mutters one of the men at the table.

Laughter erupts.

Peirce looks directly at me.

"Paul—here's where we need your help. After you hand off the relics to the right folks in Baghdad, we need for you to stay on for a while and help us get the Akbar Club off the ground—expand its membership throughout Iraq and even to the neighborhood, to Syria, Jordan, the Gulf, even Saudi ... but not Israel—it's too soon for that.

"We gotta get the Sunnis and the Shiites and the Kurds in Iraq talking to one another—even if they start out slaughtering each other—then, we have to replicate this model throughout the region.

"We know it won't be easy to get all the factions to play nice after Saddam bites the dust. State put together a real thumb-sucker of a post-invasion plan to do this, but DOD blew them off—they say we won't have the time ... got to get that oil flowing. So we're stuck with this Akbar Club bullshit.

"I'm not suggesting it's *all* up to you, Paul. This will take years ... and, believe me, we're going to be out there for years. But we need you to kick-start it in Iraq.

"You have all the chops. You're single, you know something about the other religions, you have experience working with other cultures, and I know you'll make a good impression on the members of the Club."

Then, he moves to the close.

"*Plus,* you're a Christian ... but you're not a loony-tunes Christian, if you get my drift. We think we'll have a real problem with our Christian brethren—fundamentalist missionaries—wanting to have their own invasion of Iraq right after ours.

"But the last thing we'll need is another Crusade. It's going to be tough enough to get the hajjis to stop slaughtering each other after we bust Saddam. We don't need our Christian friends in that shooting gallery!"

Finishing with a flourish, Peirce enlists mammon in the service of God.

"Let me say something else—you can essentially name your price. We're going to be relying on a lot of private contractors to help us out in Iraq. And, to put it mildly, the pay is going to be *very* good. I can't go into the specifics here, but trust me.

"Whaddaya say, Paul?"

Oil Patch North

I'm already gone. Kierkegaard's Clown and I are off to another circus. We are standing in the middle of a desolate field. In the distance we see the usual forlorn tents. As we draw closer we can read the drooping banner.

Tent No. 5: Baku and Ashgabat
Oil for One on the Cowboy Caspian!

The Clown and I are heading toward our rusty, dented taxi, which is parked at the edge of the vast refugee camp. Our driver lounges against the right front fender. He is smoking.

Young boys, dressed in old jeans and worn jerseys, kick a cloth soccer ball around the dirt yard that makes up the camp's communal square. Their mothers huddle together in groups of four or five, watching their sullen sons play. Even younger children wander about, some playing hide-and-seek in their mothers' skirts.

At the fringes of the dusty field, sunk deep in their military jackets against the chill of the late afternoon, four chain-smoking security guards, walk around in circles, their AK-47s slung over their shoulders.

The Clown and I have just emerged from a lengthy visit to one of the dirt-floored huts, where we have been listening to the sad tale of the wife of the house, who has been living there in poverty with her family of three children for twelve years. She had been ejected from her home village by Armenian immigrants who claim large chunks of western Azerbaijan as their own.

The refugee women have suffered much, but today their spirits are high. They have heard on the state radio that the Azeri government, after years of torturous negotiations with international energy companies—some from Russia and China, but by far the most from the U.S. and Europe—has just reached a "global" agreement on the recovery of oil and gas from the Caspian Sea, on whose western shore the capital city of Baku sits. These mineral riches will travel west by pipelines though Turkey to Europe, and northwest to Russia.

Now, after decades of poverty and social disintegration, the mothers' patience and trust in their government will be rewarded—too late for themselves, perhaps, but at least for their children, especially their sons, who stand most at risk from crime, drugs, and disease. They can hardly believe their good fortune, and all the cynicism that usually runs so high among the former allies of the Soviet Union seems to have been washed away by hope.

We get into the taxi—the Clown again invisible to all but me—and go back to Baku for lunch. We are headed for Clarabelle's, which has been described to me as the best restaurant in town. It is near the diplomatic and corporate enclave, where the finest villas in the city are found, and I ask the driver to circle through it before dropping me off.

He is reluctant.

"That neighborhood is not for me or a taxi like this," he says. "It's for the elite, the bosses. They might not even let us in."

"Let's try," I say. "If they give us any trouble I'll tell them that I am an American oil engineer—that should work."

The driver shrugs and heads for the enclave.

Sure enough, before we have driven more than ten yards onto the old, elegant cobblestone street running down the center of the enclave, a great-coated guard pops out of a sentry shack disguised as the entrance of a jewelry shop. Adjusting the AK-47 hanging from his shoulder and scowling sourly, he flags us down with a nightstick with a small reflective blue paddle on the end.

I take over. I poke my head out of the window and ask if he speaks English—usually a good way to seize the initiative from a self-important cop, especially one who, like this fellow, is guarding the privileged sanctuary of foreign big shots, most of whom speak nothing but English. I'm quite certain that had we been driving a better car, he would have waved us on at that point.

After a pause he tries gamely to address me in English, his initial bravado now missing.

I ask him where the American Embassy is, flashing my passport. I assume that it is nearby—they're always in the best neighborhoods. It works. He goes into an overelaborate series of directional hand signs, speaking officiously in Azeri to the driver and ignoring me. We drive on.

As we proceed slowly along, I read the discrete brass plates on each villa. First come the quasiofficial financiers of the world energy industry—the World Bank and the International Monetary Fund. Then these institutions' "customers"—the major "private" banks of the United States, Europe, China, and Japan—begin. Next come the familiar names of the major oil companies from the "Seven Sisters" club. Finally, the second-tier companies from second-tier countries from around the world, each jostling for a place in the latest "Great Game."

The Clown ends his long silence.

"Are these the guys who are going to make sure that the locals get their fair share of their country's oil revenues?"

"I guess so," I reply aloud—the driver looking around to see if I was talking to him or myself. "I don't know who else those refugee women can rely on unless it's their own government."

"Sure," the Clown scoffs, "together they'll get 'er done! They always do, don't they?"

It is three in the afternoon, and I am the only diner in Clarabelle's. The Clown sits opposite, invisible again except to me.

I never like being the only patron in a restaurant, especially a fancy one. I feel as if the waiter—and even the chef—are performing just for me, and that I am expected to show appropriate appreciation for the individual attention being lavished on me, not just dine anonymously and unmolested.

It is beginning to happen here. Soon after the waiter hands me a wine list which I had not requested, the chef appears at my table and, in broken English, reviews the "specials." I interrupt his recitation at the second item, lemon sole, and order it and a glass of the house white.

But he isn't through.

"You can't come to Baku without having some of the world's best Beluga caviar—straight from the Caspian Sea," he says, motioning to a large window giving out onto the water. "It's a special bargain here—the equivalent of eleven U.S. dollars for all you can eat. Anywhere else it would cost you several hundred dollars. Can I bring you some as an appetizer?"

"Do it!" says the Clown. "When in Rome ..."

I order the caviar, and the chef departs, smiling. In a very real way I feel that I *am* in Rome, an outpost of a modern empire no less real than Rome's. I don't dwell on what became of that empire. I wasn't around then and won't be around for the end of this one.

As I savor the caviar, my mind drifts back to the refugee women.

We spend the night in the luxurious but almost empty Grand Hotel Royale and now, at seven the next morning, the hotel's complimentary limousine is hurrying us to the port. We are trying to catch the day's only ferry across the Caspian Sea to Turkmenbashi, Turkmenistan's, and indeed, Central Asia's, only real port on the Caspian.

Turkmenbashi was known as Krasnovodsk when the Soviet Union ruled the region. But when Turkmenistan became independent on the fall of the Iron Curtain, it came under the harsh rule of a dictator who, in 1993, declared himself president for life and insisted on being called "Turkmenbashi," or "Leader of All Turkmen."

No one was particularly surprised when he gave Krasnovodsk his own new name.

Our limousine races past faded, genteel, stone houses in tree-shaded neighborhoods, sprung up during Baku's first oil boom in the early 1900s. The Clown notes rather officiously that the dominant oil baron at that time was an Armenian buccaneer named Gulbenkian. His son, Coulouste, known enviously to his rivals as "Mr. Five Percent," had formed, and taken his usual cut of, the Iraqi Petroleum Company, into which American and European oil companies had placed the Mesopotamian fields after grabbing them from the Ottoman Empire following World War I.

I think, perhaps it is just as well for poor Azeris that the West did not use then the strategy that it is using now in Iraq to bring to Iraqis a fair share of their country's natural wealth.

We stop at a red light near a small park, and the driver points out a low stone wall pockmarked with bullet holes. He says that executions took place there during the Soviet years, and that if I look closely, I can see that two "eyes" had been added. It now resembles a sinister specter staring at me like a spy.

We head down a hill that opens to a panorama of the Caspian Sea. For several miles off to the right we can see thousands of acres of disused and abandoned oil rigs, derelict and rusting, extending into the sea for perhaps half a mile. A reddish oil slick extends to the horizon. Far offshore, through the haze, we see the ghostly outlines of active drilling platforms, erected in haughty disregard of the environmental disaster festering closer to shore.

The port comes into view. We approach it by driving around a forlorn and abandoned amusement park that had once been the summertime escape for thousands of locals and vacationing Russians. Now nothing that remains works: the benches on the merry-go-round are broken and peeling; the painted ponies have stopped their perpetual race, some stuck at midpole, others higher, and others lower. For them the race is over—there are no children in sight.

The entrance to the port is some hundred yards beyond the amusement park. A large ferry is tied up at the worn wooden pier and a line of perhaps fifty vehicles—mostly canvas-covered trucks and ancient Ladas—the former Soviet Union's version of everyman's car—wait in the queue for the signal to drive aboard. Interspersed among these are perhaps ten luxury late-model Mercedes sedans, darkened windows shut tight, each sprouting at least two antennae.

Ah, I think, the southern branch of the *nomenklatura,* the oligarchs, the oil and gas barons. Business as usual.

The crossing takes two hours, and for most of it, the Clown and I lean against the port rail, gazing into the haze that is just now stubbornly beginning to lift. We are on our own, now, the hotel driver having shown us to the ferry's ticket booth and returned to the hotel. We will have to hire a taxi in Turkmenbashi to take us on to Ashgabat, Turkmenistan's capital.

Offshore oil and gas platforms litter the sea. They buzz with life as roustabouts diligently and expertly suck out the hydrocarbons that make this area the world's most coveted and contested pit stop—a contest just short of open warfare. I can almost hear the "black gold" seeping into the waters. I queasily wonder about the caviar I had had yesterday, scooped from a local sturgeon.

Two hours later we enter the harbor of Turkmenbashi. We see more hydrocarbon hyperactivity but very few—almost no—local people. Construction crews are completing the seaside termini of three oil and gas pipelines, which snake up the gradual rise leading away from the port to the southeast. Huge rounded sections of the pipelines are positioned along the route, waiting to be welded together.

A large oil refinery is hard at its work of blighting the surrounding environment. It is the start of a process which ends with the production of products which, when they are put to their intended uses, also blight the environments where they are burned.

We walk off the ferry and spend the next thirty minutes haggling with a taxi driver about taking us to Ashgabat, some two hundred kilometers away. We agree to pay him extra for his return trip, for which, he insists, he will have no paying customer.

With the Clown and I in our accustomed place for these fantasy tours—in the taxi's backseat—the taxi follows the only road into the center of the city of about sixty thousand. Again, I am struck by the almost total absence of locals. But for the fact that thousands of people live here, almost all of the visible activity is being conducted by oil- and gas-related, hard-hatted workers, most of them, it appears, foreigners employed by foreign oil companies.

We soon arrive at the town square, a vast roundabout flanked on all sides by squat, Soviet-style official buildings, each about ten stories high. Apart from the occasional farmer guiding his camel-powered cart down the middle of the road, there is almost no traffic.

A short distance further on, the Clown, who has been quietly pensive for the past hour, suddenly points to a low-lying structure covering several acres off to the side of the road. He suddenly "remembers" that Turkmenbashi is the western terminus of the Trans-Caspian Railroad and insists that we visit it, if only for a few minutes.

The railroad links the "stans" of the Caspian region together and was in place long before their dodgy airlines, all flying dangerous castoff Soviet Tupolevs, opened for business.

I am not enthusiastic but offer no resistance. I motion to the driver where to park and somehow convey to him that we will return soon to continue our journey. He looks mystified but smiles and parks the taxi.

The cavernous building is all but deserted. A half-dozen sweepers in soiled orange jumpsuits swipe halfheartedly with long-handled brooms at the cigarette butts and discarded newspapers which the quickening breeze from the open skylight scatters about. The arrival and departure boards each displays only one train, but I cannot read the Cyrillic-style lettering.

The Clown looks around anxiously, as if he is expecting someone—but there is no sign of an arriving train, or, for that matter, any train. And there appear to be no travelers in the terminal.

Then the Clown's lined face breaks into a smile. I follow his gaze and see a local man walking briskly toward us from the information kiosk in the center of the floor, about fifty yards away. He is dressed in the regional style—baggy pantaloons cinched at the waist with a length of brightly colored cloth and a loose-fitting, white collarless shirt. His head is ringed by a black-and-white checked kaffiyeh, which drops to six inches below his shoulders, down his back. As he draws closer I notice the six-inch-long ceremonial dagger thrust into his cloth belt.

I turn toward the Clown to see if he recognizes the man, but he is gone. Then stranger shouts from ten yards away, "Paul! What the hell took you so long?"

I know the voice: it is Shadow Peirce—in his best going-native colonial getup—"Shadow of Central Asia."

"I heard in Washington that you were going to have a look-see up here before heading to Baghdad. That's great! Might as well see for yourself what's goin' on up here in the 'Stans.

"How about this outfit! I don't get to wear it very often anymore.

"Hope you don't mind me taggin' along—I can show you *just* what I was talking about—the pipeline and all."

I smile weakly. "We were just checking out this old terminal before driving down to Ashgabat. A relic from the Turks and the Soviet Union, I guess."

Peirce's brow furrows, and I realize instantly that I had made a blunder. He doesn't understand my saying "we." The Clown is gone, of course, and I'm saying "we."

He lets it pass. God only knows what mental note he's taking.

"You got a car and driver outside?" he asks, a little too offhandedly, I think.

"Yes, sir!" I say, hoping my burst of matey enthusiasm would preempt his dwelling on my blunder.

"Well, let's get started—if we hustle along, we can make Ash-town in time for dinner."

We walk out to the taxi. At my insistence, Peirce climbs into the front seat next to our driver. I'm in the backseat, next to the Clown, who, right on schedule, has reappeared, grinning broadly at me.

Peirce natters on.

"You know, Paul, that little exercise we'll be putting together down in Iraq—that's just a sideshow. We'll be pumping oil out of that hellhole in no time, turn it over to the majors to divvy up, and get up here ASAP. *This* is the Big Show.

"You saw all those rigs in the sea? Then you get an idea of the scope of all of this—and see who we have to wrestle it from—if you read me, partner."

Our taxi hurries us southeast toward Ashgabat. At the start our trip the late morning sun is in our eyes, effectively blocking out much of the road ahead. But as it rises higher we can see more—but there is not much to see besides the hundreds of square miles of empty white sand desert and the occasional camel train in the shimmering distance.

Mercifully, within the first half hour, Peirce has dozed off. The Clown is still grinning, but I, too, am soon dozing fitfully.

As we approach the town of Balkanabat, a dusty commercial center and camel market, Peirce, now wide awake, jerks his head around and taps my knee to rouse me.

Pointing past the driver and out the left-side window, he says excitedly, "See those pipes over there?"

I struggle to an upright position and peer into the desert. Some two hundred yards away, laid end to end but not yet bolted together, are hundreds of pipeline sections exactly like the one we saw in the port area of Turkmenbashi.

Painted on each section are two lines of large letters. The top line appears to be in English and the bottom line in Turkmenistan's language. I ask the drive to slow down so I can try to read the English line. It says:

US Plus its Oil and Gas Partners: Moving Energy, Spreading Democracy

Peirce is wide awake and animated.

"Can you see that oil company logo between the lines? This deal is *finally* going to happen! Those pipes are aimed right at Afghanistan. Once we boot the Taliban out of there, we can run them pipes straight down to Pakistan and the Arabian Sea. From there we can sell the product anywhere we want."

I think I hear the Clown say, "... and for the Turkmen people, a new camel in every garage."

"You see, Paul," Peirce is saying, "if the oil and gas from Central Asia is flowing this way, it means it *isn't* flowing to north to Russia. And that's good. Russia doesn't need it. They've got more oil and gas than they'll ever need—even if it takes them a hundred years to recover it.

"But we *do* need it now—and down the road we don't want to be in the position of having to beg Russia for some of theirs."

An hour later we have passed the town of Gyzylarbat, and Peirce has another sight for us to see. He motions to the driver to turn right off the road onto an improved dirt road. A mile later we come upon a parking lot near an abandoned gazebo where ice cream and soft drinks are for sale. Ten or twelve cars—mostly ancient Ladas—are parked there. Young children and their parents are milling around in bathing suits, eating ice cream and walking to and from a bunker. A handrail and steps lead from the surface of the bunker down into the sand, which turns out to be an underground spring that has been turned into a swimming hole.

At Peirce's insistence, we walk down into the dank interior, sweating profusely from the humidity produced by the baking heat at the surface and the chilly water far below. We stop at the first platform, and I come close to slipping on the worn wooden steps, which are greasy from the humidity and constant traffic of the wet and barefoot swimmers.

I peer down over the railing and see that there are two more platforms between the water and us. I hear squeals and shouts of delight rising from unseen swimmers in the Stygian gloom below.

"I thought you might find this interesting," Peirce says. "For me it's a constant reminder not to become too comfortable with your surroundings in a place like this. Never in a million years would I expect to find a cold underground swimming hole in a place like this.

"It always makes me wonder what else I don't know about places like this."

As we walk back to the taxi, Peirce has another suggestion.

"I want to show you something else—then we'll go."

I follow him as he climbs to the top of the sand dune looming above the water hole's entrance.

"See that raggedy bahbwire fence?" he says, pointing to the fence about one hundred yards to the south and stretching to the east and west as far as the eye can see. "Iran is on the other side. The rest of the desert is Iran. Tehran is just a couple of hours drive from where we're standing. See how easy it would be to roll in there from here—if we have to some day? That's one reason we want to stay on the right side of the big guy here in Turkmenistan. You never know."

Dusk settles on the land as we enter Ashgabat. We drive down an empty street lined on each side by small new villas, which Peirce says have been built to house the foreign energy experts whom the president is certain will soon be flocking to his city. Each villa is built it its own kitschy style—Bavarian alpine, Brazilian art deco, Chinese pagoda, and so on. Each has a small restaurant serving cuisine to match the villa's architectural style. It's a Potemkin village with a Disney feel.

We're looking for the American log cabin villa, where Peirce is staying and where he has booked a room for me. When we arrive I see that we are its only guests.

I look around for the Clown. He is sitting on a small couch near the check-in desk, doubled up in silent, ghostly laughter.

Two hours later, after we have checked in, cleaned up, and had a dinner of rib-eye steaks, Cobb salad, baked beans, with apple pie for dessert,

Peirce asks the taxi driver, who has been given a room in the servants' quarters, to drive us around town for a while.

Once again, as in the provincial towns we had seen today, the capital was for the most part empty. There were broad and modern boulevards but few *boulevardiers*. All was modern, clean, empty, and sterile.

We turn onto the grandest boulevard of all, and in the middle distance, towering above everything else, we see the Arch of Neutrality. This gigantic Ozymandian structure sits atop a steel motorized tripod which rotates by day so that the face of the statue at the pinnacle of the monument, the Turkmenbashi himself, always faces he sun.

It's dark now, so the arch is still, but huge klieg lights play on it like those that light up the Eiffel Tower at night. I steal a glance at the Clown beside me in the taxi. He's laughing again.

The next morning, at a breakfast of pancakes and sausage, Peirce makes his final pitch to me.

"I think you can understand, Paul, how important this region is to our country, and why we're here. When we've cleared the Taliban out of Afghanistan, these pipelines will be extended to Karachi in no time. Then it's 'mission accomplished.'

"And you can play an important part in all of this—beginning in Iraq. Don't let us down, pilgrim."

Springtime in Baghdad

After a week escorting the relics to two churches in Mosul, in the north of Iraq, Father Geli and I accompany them to Our Lady of Salvation Assyrian Church, in Baghdad. They are housed in an ornate three-hundred-pound reliquary mounted on a small platform five feet above the ground. The chamber itself is three feet by five feet along its glass sides and two feet high. It is made of lacquered jacaranda wood from Brazil and is trimmed in silver. A protective dome of transparent plastic covers it.

More than one hundred Iraqis had been waiting inside the Baghdad church. Some are Christians—Chaldeans, Assyrians, Latin-rite Catholics—and some are Muslims. All are frightened. Many begin to beseech the relics from the moment the sexton wheels the reliquary to the side altar, which is bright from the blaze from two hundred candles.

Later that evening, the flow of humanity reaches flood stage. Father Geli and I keep a discreet distance from the reliquary, watching first dozens, then hundreds of prayerful Iraqis queue in the street for a chance to approach. Their faith is fierce and expressions openly emotional. Lusty singing competes with the almost shouted recitation of the rosary. Every person in the queue is pressed up close against the person ahead of him.

53

Everyone shuffles forward, six inches at a time, determined to get inside the church before its door closes.

First in Mosul, and now here, Father Geli and I have spent several hours each day watching crowds like these. He has been impressed, I'm sure, but I have been floored.

I see how Iraq's Christians have to practice their faith immersed in a sea of Muslims, many of whom are belligerently hostile to them. Perhaps even more impressive are the Muslim pilgrims. As a devout Muslim it clearly takes extraordinary courage to publicly venerate the remains of a Christian "saint" and maintain one's own religious standing in the community.

This experience—watching Christians and non-Christians alike implore Thérèse for protection and help with their lives, all of which are blighted with far more uncertainty and outright danger than my own—shakes me. Spiritually, I am true to my modern Western roots—tepid, uninvolved, "entitled." I am not reassured by the contrast with the Iraqi Thérèsians.

It is seven thirty in the morning, and while my "internal alarm clock" has already roused me, I am still in bed, half asleep. The room is small, and humidity is already seeping in, blotting up the faint stream of cool air coming from the clattering air conditioner.

Outside the door, in the hallway, I hear the steps and muffled shouts of the foreign television crews bundling their gear out into the smog-shrouded streets in search of another round of pre-invasion interviews with frightened, bewildered Iraqis.

I, too, have to get moving. Father Geli and I like to be at the churches at least thirty minutes before the doors open to the public, and it is never easy for our driver to avoid the increasing number of police roadblocks that are springing up as war draws closer. I am supposed to meet Father Geli in the lobby in less than an hour.

Forty-five minutes later I am in the rickety elevator to the lobby when my cell phone breaks into its familiar Verdi ringtone. Father Geli, I think, making sure I am on my way down. Only two or three people in Iraq know my number, and most of my calls are from him. But when I glance at the screen there is no name, and the calling number is unfamiliar to me. I have been telling myself that my creeping paranoia is probably normal in this increasingly fraught city, yet a *frisson* of apprehension chills me. I turn my back on the only other person in the elevator, push the talk key, and murmur "Yes?" into the phone, cupping it with my free hand.

"Paul?" It is a female voice—a young woman. I do not recognize it, but I like her lilting French accent.

"Yes?" I breathe, trying to sound calm.

"I'm a friend of Mr. Peirce—he gave me your number and suggested that we meet. I'm with *Medicines sans frontieres*, MSF. May I come by your hotel day after tomorrow, say about ten in the morning?"

The elevator door is opening onto the lobby, and I see Farther Geli near the main door, talking to the Iraqi driver, who has good English and doubles as an interpreter for us. The French Embassy has made the arrangements.

Father's back is to me, but the driver stares over his shoulder directly at me.

"Fine," I say into the phone, and ring off. My caller had not mentioned her name. Nor, I thought, had I given my phone number to Peirce. I couldn't have done so. A functionary from the French Embassy had handed Father and me phones on our arrival in Baghdad, and given the hostility between the French and American governments in the run-up to the war, I did not see how Peirce could have known our numbers.

I soon realize that I will have to confide something of my new plans to Father Geli. The day after tomorrow I will have to leave him alone in church with the relics.

Father Geli is clearly distracted by something else, which he wants to impart urgently. He says that the French Embassy has heard that the American bombing will begin very soon, and the ambassador does not want to endanger the relics by continuing the church vigils. She has ordered that the relics be flown immediately to their next scheduled stop, Cairo.

Naturally, says Father, he will be leaving on the same plane with the relics. He has already notified the papal nuncio and French ambassador in Cairo to expect them ahead of schedule.

Father Geli urges me to leave with him. The bombing will close the airport and make any later departure by air impossible and by auto extremely hazardous.

My mind is racing.

I certainly should leave Iraq before the bombs begin to fall, and this new turn of events offers me a face-saving way to do it. I know that no one in Washington—I am thinking of Peirce—could really second-guess my decision. Officially, there is nothing more for me to do here. But still, I want to stay on for at least a couple of days. I want to meet Peirce's friend and learn her real role in Iraq and what part, if any, she might be playing in the Akbar Club.

There is something else going on with me. I am catching war fever. I am being swept into a toxic brew of excitement, danger, and camaraderie. I'm experiencing the narcotic mental clarity that always precedes the horror and stench of actual combat and killing—the realities that seldom make the evening news. I won't call this fever patriotism. I oppose this war—oppose it in every way. But it is going to be "big" and, I tell myself, I want to be a "disinterested observer," exposing myself to just as much danger as I dare during the day and, in my mind, swapping stories at night over drinks in the hotel bar with the big-time journalists and television anchors. They have war fever, too, and are already steaming into the doomed city for their next death fix.

All of these thoughts race through my mind.

"I have some personal matters to attend to before I go," I mutter to Father Geli. I hope that my demeanor at least suggests that I'd already been in touch with some shadowy American operatives on the ground in Baghdad—that I might be a "player," however minor, in the grand and grisly drama that was about to unfold. "I'll catch up with you in Cairo in a day or two."

Obviously preoccupied with the day ahead, Father Geli cannot have cared less about my excuses.

"Suit yourself," he snaps and heads out the door for our car, the driver, and I following close behind him.

Two mornings later I am in a taxi bound for Baghdad College, in a distant suburb. The driver clutches a flimsy piece of paper containing directions in Arabic. When I had asked the hotel concierge to write the note for me, I found his protracted stare unsettlingly inquisitive.

Father Geli has flown to Cairo with the relics as planned, and Peirce's contact, the French girl, has called me with a change of plans for our rendezvous. Rather than meet me at the hotel, she now wants me to come to the college, where, she says, her office has been relocated in anticipation on the bombing. It is assumed that the Americans will spare places like schools and hospitals, especially if they are on the outskirts of the city.

She had given me her name—Marthe Zanta—but, again, our conversation had been brief.

Soon my taxi is in the ramshackle heart of Sadr City, Baghdad's sprawling Shiite slum. Pushcarts, bicycles, and decrepit trucks and cars stand gridlocked in a long line from the intersection three hundred yards ahead of us. The distant traffic light turns from red to green and back again, yet we can't move. Vehicles crossing the intersection from the street up ahead ignore the light as blatantly as the cars in our queue. Beggars, many of them children, go from car to car hawking bottled water, snacks, newspapers, and an endless variety of worn and faded items that I cannot identify.

Women ranging in age from the very young to the very old, babies on their hips, hold their free hands out for alms. Many of the babies are crippled or diseased. When rebuffed, the women fade away with a smile, leaving you to wonder what the effects of your refusal will be for yourself, either in this world or the next.

A foul stench arises from the rivulets of greenish wastewater that run along the gutters. Fractious drivers shout and gesticulate at each other in an aggressive assertion of shared misery, which simmers in the humidity and acrid fumes.

The college compound is large—perhaps two hundred yards long and one hundred wide—all enclosed by a six-foot-tall stucco and wood wall. Just outside the wall are thick stands of towering cedar trees, giving the place a feeling of privacy, a tattered exclusivity.

Arching over the main gate is a sign in the shape of a crescent moon: *Baghdad College—A Jesuit High School.* Beneath these words, in Arabic script, is a motto which the taxi driver translates as "Do What You Are Doing."

The compound itself is unpaved. Clouds of reddish dust swirl into the air as small groups of students—teenaged boys, all smartly dressed in school blazers, ties, and gray slacks—shuffle between the chapel at one end of the compound and the large classroom building at the other.

Scrawny date palms dot the interior space. One of them stands out from the rest. It is in the middle of the compound, ancient and bent, really just a large shrub. But its shade is dark and cool, and every pigeon and small bird in the compound huddles beneath its sheltering branches, cooing and chirping in a blissful Babel of birdsong.

There is something incongruous about the place. Perhaps it is the presence of young boys growing up in a school that is not just old but seems to reverberate with the ghosts of the clashing ideologies that the Jesuits—who, I learn later, had founded the school but were expelled from Iraq years ago—have tried to reconcile. It seems to me that those ghosts are still here.

I dismiss the driver and enter the classroom building, looking for room 202, where I am at last to meet Marthe Zanta. A directory in Arabic and English notes that the Akbar Club is meeting there. I climb the broad curved stairway, find the room, and go in.

It is a typical classroom, four lines of student desks extending from the front of the room to back, bare whiteboards on all four walls, and, at the front, a teacher's desk on a slightly raised platform. The only unusual touch is a large oval table next to the teacher's desk.

Five people—three men and two women—are seated around the oval table. In front of each of them is a small plastic bottle of drinking water and in the middle of the table stands a large straw basket full of cookies and the colorful, delicate, spun-sugar sweets found throughout the Middle East.

Two of the men are engaged in a spirited, even rancorous, dialogue, in English—but I cannot immediately make out what they were discussing.

At first no one seems to notice me. But then the young woman who is sitting at one rounded end of the table—is she chairing the discussion?—rises and comes over to greet me. In her late twenties, she is of medium height, with a broad, open face framed by short bangs, small earrings, and a strong chin. Her curly brown hair is shoulder length, and she wears an ornately layered silk blouse topped by a round, ruffled white collar, and a long cotton skirt.

She is attractive but not strikingly beautiful in the conventional sense. Yet her face exudes an almost tangible heat—an intense magnetism that seems to arise from some inner urgency.

"*Bon jour!*" she says, I'm Marthe Zanta."

Her voice is soft, and her gaze bores right through me. "You're Paul, aren't you? Thanks for coming."

Behind her, the discussion at the oval table proceeds. The four remaining participants are all talking at once in an incomprehensible free-for-all whose volume has increased since I had arrived.

Marthe asks them to desist for a moment.

"I think you know our little group here is called the Akbar Club," she says, turning back to me "It was organized a month ago at the Holy Father's request. Our discussions have been lively."

Marthe's open disclosure of the club's genesis, mentioned in such an offhanded manner, brings me up short. Of course, I know that the pope was the prime mover behind this strange group, but if Marthe is, in fact, working, however loosely, with U.S. intelligence—and how else would Peirce know her?—does that mean that the pope has thrown his fancy hat into the middle of Iraq's very dangerous geopolitical cesspool?

The pope certainly knows that Thérèse's relics have been in Iraq, but now Father Geli has bolted for Cairo and taken the relics with him. Perhaps Geli knows Marthe, or at least knows that she is playing this double game, which he wanted no part of.

My suspicions now at the boil, I have another dark thought. Perhaps I have been the CIA's pawn in all of this from the very beginning, in Port Tobacco, when Frank Stefano had first introduced me to Geli. The French and the American governments were barely on speaking terms then over the impending war and that hadn't changed. Perhaps the French government had already conspired with the pope to work together in Iraq to blunt the invasion's inevitably disastrous effects on the Iraqi people.

Marthe must have sensed my alarm.

"Paul, our little club is not political—it's spiritual!"

"It's an effort to put something holy in place—here in Iraq—in place of bloodshed and suffering of innocent people."

She goes on.

"I think you know that when the American president sought the pope's blessing for his invasion of Iraq, the pope refused his request. But he also saw that war was inevitable. So he did not give up on the matter—he suggested that if the president was determined to attack Iraq, then he might want to do something positive, too.

"He asked the president to start something here in Iraq, in the midst of the inevitable terror and agony, which might start a *spiritual* fire, especially in the Muslim world. That would be the fire of love, which has gone out in so many places. He thought that by carefully choosing a small group of people from the Abrahamic faiths, Christians, Muslims, and Jews, regardless of gender or race, but that have already been touched by love, these people would be able to create some common ground of faith that could be replicated elsewhere very quickly!"

"Yes, I heard about it in the States," I mutter.

"And the first thing we're doing," Marthe continues, "is to try to rediscover the common thread of the Abrahamic faiths. We want to have compassion for each other's faith, to put ourselves in each other's spiritual shoes, if you like, because all three of the faiths are grounded in love, not hatred and violence. Although if you look around the world today, that might seem like a foolish statement!

"But the pope is convinced that the Abrahamic faiths are not essentially about fierce justice and retribution being brought down on their own people or people of other faiths. The pope sees God's justice as tempered by love—a love that has no place for crusades, suicide martyrdoms, beheadings, or ritual shunning of outsiders.

"So, he told the Americans that if they must go to war in Iraq and in other places around the world—if for now their fear has conquered their love—at least make some effort to rediscover the ground that is common to the Abrahamic faiths. Rediscover love!

"That's what we're about with the Akbar Club. We're looking for love."

I play along. "How were you all chosen for this group—does the pope know you all?"

"No," she replies, "he chose only Father Carvalho," glancing at the white man at the table. The other two were black and brown.

"Father Carvalho is a Jesuit from Brazil—which has more Catholics than any other country in the world, as well as millions of other Christians, animists, and who knows what else! But one thing Brazil does not have is apathy. There, people live their faith with enthusiasm, and as far as the pope is concerned, it is this kind of enthusiasm that will rejuvenate Christianity around the world—including, of course, the Catholic Church.

"Father Carvalho had some help from others in the Vatican in finding the rest of us. But the pool of possibilities was not large. We all had to be here in Iraq already, doing other things. It was organized quite quickly.

"I was suggested by your friend Mr. Peirce. It seems that your president wanted to make some sort of response to the pope's suggestion, so he said he'd ask his staff to come up with some way to involve an American. Eventually, it fell to Mr. Peirce, who was already planning to come to Baghdad, to follow through. He asked me to participate. We know each other from my work in *Medicines sans frontieres*, the volunteer medical organization. I had hoped to be assigned to Hanoi, but *MSF* sent me here instead. Mr. Peirce seemed to know you would be joining us."

"And my role in all of this is…."

Marthe, again. "You're our big *American!* We're counting on you to help us where we can't go ourselves, to listen to us, and to help us spread the word. *Will* you help us?"

"You can count on me," I reply, trying for a tone of knowing half-seriousness, just in case this is all some kind of joke.

Marthe is still speaking—in a professional tone of voice—a tone that says, "This is serious. Pay attention."

"His Holiness wants to show the world that the West and the Arabs can draw on their common roots and work together—that war is not the answer to our problems.

"This has been tried before. Jesuit priests founded this very school, Baghdad College, many years ago. They built something here that lasted for many years because it brought something valuable to Iraq—and to the Middle East.

"So the pope turned to a Jesuit to restart the process and to remind both the West and the Iraqis of the possibilities for cooperation that have been around for centuries but have been forgotten.

"I give you our leader, Father Hector Carvalho."

Marthe again turns to the oval table.

This august worthy is in his midseventies, tall, thin, stooped, with an aquiline nose, sharp features, and close-set pale blue eyes. He is dressed in a tropical white shirt and trousers and holds a crisp Panama hat in his elegant, long-fingered hands. His patrician appearance and aloof air suggest disillusioned sophistication, a pensive world-weariness. He reminds me rather of a praying mantis—angular, spare, delicate, still—somewhat mysterious.

My first thought is that he might be Marthe's "special friend"—perhaps a postmodern clerical *roué*—showing her Mesopotamian wonders with an aggressive erudition that he hoped would compensate for other, perhaps less-robust, capacities.

My musings bring me up short. Am I becoming possessive of a girl I have just met? Am I retreating back into my defensive, self-protective crouch? It occurs to me that this is just the sort of insecurity, parading as self-assurance, which drove Jenny away.

Marthe continues to talk, but my revived memories of Jenny are drowning her out. Once again, the familiar waves of hurt, pain, regret, and anger sweep over me, snapping the flimsy branch of denial that I have been so tenaciously clinging to since she left me.

Marthe doesn't really remind me of Jenny. She seems to be a girl with a mission—what else can explain her being here in this dangerous country, at this rundown school, with these strange characters?

No, she is nothing like Jenny. Jenny didn't have a mission. But then, I wasn't sure I ever really knew her. I thought I loved her, and I thought she loved me and wanted to walk down together on a path toward some gauzy, undefined destination called "happiness." If Jenny had a mission, that would've been it. I had thought that that was my mission, too. But it wasn't.

I was walking down a path by myself, never really knowing where I was headed or who, if anyone, I wanted to go with me. When Jenny realized this, she said good-bye. No histrionics, very few tears, just a stoic resignation that had pierced my carefully constructed façade of self-sufficiency more effectively than a knife to my gut.

Marthe is clearly on her own path, and she knows where it is taking her. And when I finally met her, when I heard her speak, I was immediately drawn to her.

The Akbar Club Meets

*F*ather Carvalho rises and begins to speak in an even, languid tone.

"First—why do we call it the Akbar Club?

"Four hundred years ago, a Mughal ruler of India, Akbar the Great, tried to synthesize three of the world's major religions—Islam, Hinduism, and Christianity—into a coherent philosophy. He was a Muslim, of course, but he was an unusual Muslim. For instance, he softened the harsher aspects of Islam with music and dance, which he had seen performed by Sufis, a mystical sect of Islam.

"But he was amazingly tolerant of all religions. He built a combination palace and fort outside Agra, in the north of the country. Inside the fort he built a special building where he could listen to his nine palace theologians debate the merits of the separate religions.

"He also built separate sections for his wives, who included Muslims, Hindus, and Christians. The first of his two Christian wives was the daughter of a Portuguese merchant in Gujarat, in western India.

"Akbar coveted Goa, which the Portuguese had recently acquired, but his interest in Christianity was real. He was impressed by Christian visitors from Kerala, in southern India, and he even considered converting to Catholicism but was dissuaded from doing so by conservative imams.

"Toward the end of his life he founded his own religion whose tenets were drawn from all religions. Believers wore white and worshipped the sun.

"Here's the point," said Father. "There exists in this world an immense quantity of goodness and beauty which, I believe, will eventually be fulfilled in Christ. But, meanwhile, it exists, and we Christians must feel a fellowship with those of other faiths who see that goodness and beauty, too, if we want to be fully Christian and assimilate it to God.

"However difficult it will be, I think we must nurture that sense of fellowship with Islam.

"Each of us here in the Akbar Club has his or her own ideas on how this might be accomplished. Let me tell you mine."

There seemed little chance of stopping him, I think. But I am also becoming intrigued.

Father Carvalho continues.

"I am a scientist, a biologist, but my career began at a time when Rome was still very suspicious of science.

"The Church had made a big mistake in condemning Galileo and knew it. Ever since then it has struggled to live with the consequences of that mistake: a reconfirmed reputation as an institution more interested in maintaining literal interpretations of the Old Testament than accommodating scriptural interpretation to scientific evidence.

"The Church was fearful that openly accepting scientific reality would also mean accepting the scientific method as the only path to truth—and that, they thought, would undermine the more important truths that had been revealed not by science but by Revelation, the Incarnation, and the Resurrection—truths that people live by even more than by scientific truths."

This fellow is used to preaching and obviously loves doing so to captive audiences. Nothing in his austere tone encourages interruption.

Should I be taking notes? I wonder.

"God gave us science," Carvalho goes on, "just as He gave us everything we have. I had developed some theories on how evolution was part of God's plan for mankind's journey through life to ultimate salvation—a journey far more complex than Darwin's discoveries suggested. I had trouble with Rome because they did not have the language they needed to accurately describe mankind's—and the universe's—journey, and they distrusted the language I was offering them."

I can't help myself. "So, did Darwin miss the evolution boat?"

My flippancy does not distract him.

"No, he didn't," said Father Carvalho, managing a condescending smile.

"He caught the evolution boat, but it was a small boat. It was the only boat he could see at the dock at that time, and he boarded it. And it is a good thing he did. Biological evolution and natural selection are facts, and biological diversity in a population arises from random genetic mutations based on their ability to reproduce."

I struggle to follow him but am not wholly succeeding.

He does not wait for me.

"Most of Darwin's disciples, the Neo-Darwinians, have sailed that boat to many fascinating and wondrous places, and they have given all of us a stunning tour of nature's evolution. But some of Darwin's noisiest shipmates—I call them Uber-Darwinians—want to load too much cargo on the little evolution boat. They think that it can carry both mankind's scientific *and* nonscientific cargo—provide answers to *all* of mankind's questions about creation.

"They do not realize that evolution is not just about the development and adaptation of physical species. It is also about the evolution of *human consciousness*. In other words, evolution is occurring in the *spiritual* realm as well as the physical realm. And just as evolution drives physical species forward to some *unknown* destination, so is the human consciousness evolving—but toward a destination that more and more of us believe we can make out in the misty distance. We certainly do *not* know where evolution is taking the physical species.

"So the Uber-Darwinians miss a very important part of the evolution story—and today, more and more of them realize their unhappy mistake. This makes many of them uneasy—even hostile. They are not happy that *their* evolution boat has begun to sink under the load they've placed on it."

"What the hell has all of this got to do with the Akbar Club?" I asked myself. Blind evolution or "intelligent design"—these weren't the issues facing Iraq and the West.

Carvalho keeps right on talking, extremely pleased to be so deeply into his maritime metaphor.

"The Uber-Darwinians were all on Darwin's evolution boat when another boat appeared on the horizon. That boat was bigger and older than Darwin's. For hundreds of millions of years it had been plowing through waters whose currents run deeper and stronger than those which Darwin's little boat skims over, tacking back and forth depending on which way evolution's breezes are blowing at any given time. Unlike Darwin's boat, the older, larger boat had a longer keel and more space—space for a 'captain' who allowed evolution to steer the boat but did not announce the boat's destination, route, or time of arrival."

How many times had Carvalho given this speech, I wonder.

"On the larger boat, the captain's hand is not on the wheel. He—or she—is focused on a reality more fundamental than the mechanics of physical evolution—a reality that is revealed only to those who have the courage to ask the most obvious questions: '*Who* built the boat? *Who* launched it? *When* was it launched?' When rational people—people who are guided by reason—ask those questions, they must conclude that there is a force, a power, a 'captain,' if you will, who built the boat and launched it. Boats don't just appear out of nothing. One can't go from nothing to something. Only God can do that.

"How long is the voyage, and what is its destination? We'll have to wait and see. We've been sailing on this bigger boat for several eons now and perhaps we'll sail on for many more. Some Uber-Darwinians seem to think that the voyage will never end; others think, geologically speaking, it will end tomorrow. Still others seem to think that their part of the voyage will end when they die, and that's all they know for certain. But some of us have met the captain and are content to let him—or her—stay on duty until we reach port."

Still unchastened, I venture a question.

"Will the Uber-Darwinians ever move over to the captain's boat?"

"Who knows?" Carvalho replies. "They have invested everything they have—their egos, their professional reputations, their entire self-image—in the little boat's cargo, and many don't think they can afford to switch boats now. But even as their own boat founders under its heavy load, many refuse to abandon ship. It's almost as if they are determined to go down with their boat, themselves victims of rules very much like those that govern natural selection.

"Sadly, perhaps this time it is *they* who are the species being randomly selected for professional extinction. We all have free will, of course, so the choice is theirs. And because they are rational people, we can only hope they choose rationally.

"But even though many of them suspect this, as they themselves know better than most, no one can yet say for certain why some species survive and others disappear."

At last I think I know where Carvalho is going with all this. His bit of the Akbar Club is becoming clear to me.

He seems to be nearing the end of his disquisition.

"Today, even Darwin himself would not be found on board that little boat with the Uber-Darwinians. He was an agnostic, not an atheist. He once wrote to a Harvard naturalist: 'I feel most deeply that the whole subject is too profound for the human intellect. A dog might as well speculate on the mind of Newton....'"

"It's not a question of evolution!"

Sarah Feld is seated across from Father Carvalho at the oval table. Her dark eyes glare from beneath dark brows—and she is angry. She is perhaps four years older than Marthe but has none of her warm appeal. She is almost a frumpy anorexic, wearing a nondescript peasant dress, her frizzy black hair falling to earlobe level on each side of her pinched, sharp face. Wire-rimmed glasses slide midway down her narrow nose. She wears no makeup. Indeed, her most striking characteristic is her utter unconcern with fashion and personal adornment.

Her intellect glistens like Mack's knife.

"It's not about how species develop—it's not about how one species survives and another one dies ... it's about *love*—and how we, the human species, find it and give it! The rest is all mechanics!"

Father Carvalho stares at her—obviously not pleased at having his life work so characterized. He takes a deep breath, but before he can defend himself, Marthe intervenes.

"Sarah, before you say anything more, please tell Paul something about yourself—where you're coming from."

Father Carvalho shoots Marthe a wintry glance but withdraws for the moment, sinking back into his chair.

Sarah herself seems annoyed at Marthe's suggestion. She clearly wants to make her point and not pause for a biographical detour. She seems eager to tangle with Carvalho. But she stands down.

"I am a Jew, born in Paris. My work—my vocation—has been finding holiness among working people, those who do life's truly hard work. I find I can best practice my vocation through Christianity," she mumbles. Her words including all of us in a collective guilt through an unspoken consensus.

There is an embarrassed stirring in the room. No one seems prepared for such unflinching candor. Marthe jumps into the breach.

"I think the same could be said today for much of Islamic and Christian spirituality, too! That's what we want to change!"

Sarah Feld ignores her.

"As a girl, I identified closely with the working poor—I was motivated by the same compassion that drove many French religious and Christian laypeople in the 1930s and '40s to organize themselves to help the poor. You may have heard of the French Confederation of Christian Workers, or the Young Christian Farmers. Many priests and nuns wore work clothes and worked alongside men and women in the factories and fields to share their lives and, in many cases, re-Christianize them. Some even married.

"In doing this kind of hard work, they tried to show solidarity with the workers and energize the French church, which badly needed it.

"My friends and I tried to do something like this, too, but we hit a brick wall. We couldn't get jobs in factories, no matter how menial. So we considered other routes—for example, joining groups like the Taize Community, Communion and Liberation, and Sant'Egidio."

She trails off. Father Carvalho and I begin to shift uncomfortably, each of us rummaging around in our respective bags of practiced small talk for some graceful way to break the silence. Marthe is serene, showing no hint of unease.

The two other persons at the table, to whom I had not yet been introduced, sit impassively. One of them appears to be an imam. Short, pudgy, and in his fifties, he wears a full-length garment and a tightly wrapped gray turban on his head. Black-rimmed glasses and a close-cropped frame his jowly features, graying beard. He stares straight ahead.

The other person is an elderly black man whose appearance resembles that of a career diplomat at the United Nations. Tall, graying, and paunchy, he wears a black, three-piece business suit and has an air of distinguished reserve.

Sarah Feld finally picks up her narrative.

"My friends saw beauty in these groups. Beauty in what we could contribute of ourselves to the poor, and beauty in each other."

She lapses into silence again. Then, thirty seconds later:

"People long for beauty, and when they see it in a person they may think that they love that person, but what they love is that person's beauty. No one, no matter how beautiful, can give someone else what that person truly seeks. Only God can satisfy that longing.

"For myself, I came to realize what Dostoyevsky meant when he wrote that the world will be saved by beauty."

Again, Sarah Feld pauses for several seconds. Then she says, "I didn't join any of the groups I just mentioned. Instead, I took a job teaching history in the countryside, near Lyon.

"But I couldn't forget the poor. I organized a debate with a Catholic priest, a rabbi, an imam, and an atheist, much like this group. The debate's proposition was, 'God Is Found Only in the Shopping Mall: True or False?' It was a lively discussion, but when my supervisor at the school heard about it, my teaching contract was not renewed. So I joined *Medicines sans frontieres,* and was posted here, where I met Marthe."

Father Carvalho strikes.

"I must say, Miss Feld" he says, resorting to a well-honed tone of professional condescension, "I don't quite see the connection between your spiritual sensibilities—your inner journey, if you will—and evolution."

His words hold a full measure of practiced dismissal.

Sarah Feld immediately returns fire.

"Of course you don't! There isn't any!

"*How* we humans got here, and *how* we evolved is an interesting *scientific* question perhaps, but it misses the main point, which is *love*. We *are* here because God *loves* us. We, in turn, are looking for love in all kinds of places—and that search is really a longing that God infused in us from the beginning—a longing to be reunited with him.

"And *that's* what *this* club is all about. How *all* of us—Christians, Muslims, Jews, and others—can find that love and throw out everything else that divides us."

Impressively, Father Carvalho does not miss a beat.

"But don't you see, Miss Feld, that evolution—'*how* we got here,' as you put it—is *itself* a sign of God's love! By his love he is moving us—humanity—to higher levels of consciousness every day. And those *mechanics,* if you will, show that God has tied our *spiritual* advancement to the earth's *physical evolution* through some kind of 'cosmic DNA,' if you will. And *that's* a messy process—a chaotic process that we see today right here in Iraq and in countless other places around the world.

"Instability and strife may just mean that that process—evolution of our own species—is speeding up."

Sarah Feld looks furiously impatient. She regards Father as if any coherence his argument might contain is defeated by its exhausting efforts to climb out of the gullies of garrulity in which it is mired.

Father Carvalho takes instant advantage of her preoccupied silence, remaining firmly perched on his elaborately carved but inherently wobbly chair of evolutionary theory.

"In the evolution of species, it is instability, not stability, that moves physical creation to a higher level. This instability is reflected in the battle of species to survive. But in the parts of the universe's evolution that are *not* governed *only* by Darwinian rules of evolution (and I'm talking about human beings), war and chaos—social instability—can also signal that momentous spiritual changes are on the way.

"Strangely, God can sometimes seem closer to us when there is danger. Many soldiers—and even some foreign journalists I've talked to here—have experienced this.

"In any event, God may be found in both joy and suffering. He is *not* found in quiet times. We must see instability as a sign that mankind's *spiritual* evolution is advancing.

"In believing this, we must take a courageous leap—our faith in God's divine providence—his love—assures us that he is at work in the cosmos and will not in the end throw us on a cold cosmic slagheap. We must embrace the future, not fear it. We must be daring if we wish to enter the kingdom.

"Be daring, Miss Feld! That's what we need … a daring soul! Be bold!"

Sarah Feld remains speechless. No one else speaks either.

Finally, having collected herself, Sarah Feld hisses, "Father, if God's 'cosmic DNA' involves the kind of chaos we have here in Iraq today, I want nothing to do with it. To me, we humans are regressing, not evolving to some higher spiritual plane. We're making a living hell for people who had nothing to do with 9/11. We're wreaking havoc on innocent people, especially the poor. *This* is an advance from World War II? From the Holocaust?"

This time, Father Carvalho is speechless.

I try to conciliate.

"Father, what if you're wrong? What if those who are causing so much suffering in the world have nothing to do with an evolution of the spirit? Suppose their own personal DNA has no connection with anything but evil. Suppose it has no connection whatever with some cosmic DNA. Aren't they bound for hell when they die—completely unevolved, spiritually?"

"Perhaps so, Paul," he replied softly. "I'll leave that to God.

"But I like what a colleague of mine once told me how he answered that question. He said, 'As a priest I am required to believe in the existence of hell, but I am *not* required to believe that anyone is there.'

"Perhaps our only hell is right here, right now."

The austere black man finally speaks up. His voice is soft, his accent Oxbridge.

"Let me make my modest contribution, if I may." His courtesy is elaborate.

"My name is Augustin Barry. I have been Senegal's ambassador to Iraq for three years. Senegal is a former French colony on Africa's west coast. Most of the slaves who were shipped from Africa to America sailed in chains from my country."

I know Senegal. It borders The Gambia on three sides.

"Senegal is more than 95 percent Muslim," Barry goes on, "but my family was Christian. I was fortunate. I received a good education and learned to survive—even thrive—in that alien culture. I was able to see where Christianity and Islam might meet. I recognized that the essential problem is the problem of God. I understood that the god of the Muslim, like the god of the African animist, is *personal*. I found that god in Christianity, too, a God in whom all centers of love converge.

"Christians and Muslims will succeed in again finding that convergence of love only if, together, they try again to build *something new* from that love, not just try to avert catastrophe."

Marthe breaks in.

"I would think that the chances of Christians and Muslims in the West building something new today would be very difficult. There is such bitterness, such mistrust."

Barry responds, not pleased to have an interlocutor wander unbidden into his recitation.

"I lived in France for many years. And I became spiritually numb at first. I found many fellow Africans in France but almost no trace of Africa's human warmth in Paris's cold, cobbled streets.

"One day, desperate in my loneliness, I wrote a poem. I was trying to dull my emptiness by putting it into words. I have forgotten most of it but could try to recite some of it, if you like."

"Please do!" It is Marthe. The other three mutter their polite but unenthusiastic agreement.

"Thank you, Marthe," says Barry, pointedly ignoring the rest of us. "I think any African man living in France today—and there are many thousands of them—would know what I mean."

Barry begins his recitation, slowly, sonorously. He takes us to Paris, but not to the City of Light whose intimate ambiance absorbs all alien influences, but the Paris whose intoxicating cocktail of casual sensuality and earnest artifice has for centuries drawn naïve strivers who would taste the delights of the former by affecting the pose of the latter.

Barry's African in Paris sees or dreams about a woman—Is she black? Is she white?—in the *metro,* in church, in a sunset. Her voice speaks to him softly; her exotic fragrance suffuses his senses. He is sick with a carnal longing whose roots are sunk deep in his humanity and culture.

His longing is in vain. It cannot be sated in Paris. But the lure of the eternal feminine won't abate: the woman obsesses him; he cannot escape her.

I wonder, is this the kind of attraction to the beautiful that Sarah Feld was talking about?

Then Barry makes an abrupt leap from the eternal feminine to the concretely practical.

"My question is this. How can we translate all these intimations of love—Father Carvalho's, Miss Feld's, my own—into something that we can *touch* here and now? How can we do something with all of this longing, all of this love, to help the poor here and now ... to help ourselves?"

Out of the corner of my eye I catch a brief glimpse of Kierkegaard's Clown in the back of the room. He pumps his fist as if to say, "Right on!"

Barry continues.

"The president of my country has recently proposed a rational way to start to do this in Africa—a way in which oil revenues can be fairly shared among the oil companies and the people, who are starving. This is a way the West can actually *show* love for the poor."

And then slyly: "I'll keep you posted on the reactions of the oil companies."

Marthe turns to the only person in the group who has not uttered a word.

"Imam, would you like to say how you happen to be here with us?"

He does not appear enthusiastic at the prospect of joining the free-for-all. From his body language I have the impression that the rancor has displeased him. Indeed, I think that he has been in some sort of trance.

But he begins.

"My name is Ashraf Khalifeh. I am a member of the Mevlevi Sufi branch of Islam. Father Carvalho mentioned Sufis.

"Of all the branches of Islam, we Sufis have the reputation of being the most open to other faiths and to other mystical practices. Our own mysticism is represented in our dance, the *sema,* which most non-Muslims know as the dance of 'whirling dervishes.'

"In our *sema* we seek to put our egos aside by putting our bodies through the whirling—we follow our minds and spirits toward the Perfect, toward truth, toward love. And, if we succeed, after the *sema* our minds and our spirits return to this world to love and serve all creation, not just the *umma,* the community of Muslims, but all peoples of all faiths."

He says that the sayings of Sufi mystics can be as inscrutable to Westerners as those of the Zen masters. But he stresses that Christians who had plumbed their *own* faith's mysticism were not so uncomprehending.

I press him for some examples. He is ready.
"Ibn al-Arabi said:

I—God—am known by no one but thee,
just as thou existest only by Me.
He who knows thee, knows Me
although no one knows Me.
And thus thou also art known to no one.

"Other sayings Sufis revere are, *Sufism is essence without form …* and *The Sufi is he who's thought keeps pace with his foot.*
"But the best-known Sufi mystic today is the poet Rumi, who was born in Persia, now Iran, in the thirteenth century. His writings are read throughout the world, even now. About death he wrote,

Your fear of death is really fear of yourself:
see what it is from which you are fleeing!
'Tis your own ugly face, not the visage of death:
your spirit is like the tree, death like the leaf.

"You can well imagine how our version of Islam has got us into difficulties today, when radical Islam is on the rise. Indeed, we Sufis have been banned and persecuted in many Muslim areas over the centuries.
"But like the rest of you in the club, I am basically optimistic about the long-term future of the Abrahamic religions coming together on the basic truths that we all recognize. That's why I'm here. We must begin again somewhere. Why not here? Why not now?"
Marthe speaks.
"How did you find your way here? You're not Iraqi, are you?"
"No," the imam replies. "Like Rumi, I am from Afghanistan, from the northern city of Mazar-i-Sharif. Many years ago, when the warlords began suppressing Sufis and all non-radical sects of Islam, my family and I had to flee for our lives, just as our predecessors were forced to flee the Mongol invasions of India generations before.
"We went first to Persia with the intention of settling there, but I found its religious practices too rigid. We were uncomfortable there as practicing Sufis so we moved on to Baghdad several years ago.

"There was once a thriving Sufi tradition here—pacifist and mystical—and I wanted to be a part of it. However, it couldn't last. First, Saddam and his Baathist followers persecuted Sufis, and then, of course, this coming invasion is contrary to everything Sufis have always believed. It's against truth and love.

"But my family and I have decided to stop running. We're staying here, come what may, and I will try my best to make the Akbar Club a success."

Again, Marthe intervenes.

"Imam, do you really believe we can make it work?"

"We must try," he replies.

"As a matter of fact, centuries ago in Spain, in Andalusia, a fusion of Christianity and Islam developed. People called it the *convivencia*—the 'living together.' Another example occurred in the 1300s in the Ottoman Empire. There, for about a century, both religions were often proclaimed as one. Later, a serious attempt to unite the two creeds was made, based on a common mystical love of God that obliterated all superficial differences.

"Both movements eventually fell to a resurgent Islamic militancy, but I reject the notion that a spiritual fusion between Christianity and Islam—and, yes, even Judaism—is impossible. Such an eventuality would take heroic efforts on all sides, of course, but for God, nothing is impossible."

A silence of three or four minutes fell on the group. Then Imam Khalifeh broke it.

"I wouldn't say that Muslims share *everything* with Christians and Jews—how could they? But they are part of the same family of believers. Indeed, when Christians look beyond the desperation of Islam's disaffected fanatics, they see some familiar things.

"For instance, near the Taj Mahal there is a sixteenth-century Mughal monument. Over the archway there is an inscription—I can't recall the exact words—that attributes to Jesus a quotation to the effect the world endures but an hour, and we humans should spend it praying.

"Now a couple of things struck me about that quotation—apart, of course, from seeing Jesus being quoted on a Muslim monument.

"First, after Jesus's name, the sculptor carved the words Muslims reserve for the Prophet Mohammed—'May peace be upon him.'

"Secondly, the sculptor identified Jesus as the 'son of Mary'—quite remarkable.

"Now the quotation may or may not be Jesus's words—they don't appear in the New Testament. But if they were his words, what Christian could argue with them?

"And who can argue that Christianity and Islam have absolutely no basis for reconciliation?

"Of course, Muslims do not reject freedom, as we so often hear from the West these days. Much less does Islam require the version of jihad that radical Muslims advocate. The Koran says paradise awaits someone who becomes a martyr for Allah, someone who is killed by *another* while defending Islam. The Koran *condemns* suicide and the killing of innocents. Such things are perversions of Islam, just as they are perversions of Christianity and Judaism."

There is silence in the room, but this time it isn't an embarrassed silence. The imam's message—and the manner in which he delivered it—seems to be comforting, not threatening.

Ashraf Khalifeh then enhances the new harmony.

"Father Carvalho, you might be interested in knowing that Rumi even had opinions on evolution that I believe are consistent with your own. He wrote:

I died as mineral and became a plant,
I died as plant and rose to animal,
I died as animal and was a man.
Why should I fear? When was I less by dying?
Yet once more I shall die as man, to soar
With the angels blest; but even from angelhood
I must pass on: all except God doth perish.
When I have sacrificed my angel soul,
I shall become what no mind e're conceived.
Oh, let me not exist! for Non-existence
Proclaims in organ tones, 'To Him we shall return.'"

The room is calm, the mood reflective. But the mood changes abruptly when Khalifeh begins to speak again.

"I have a serious warning. Unless the West and Islam can fill their souls with something other than what they are filled with now—something *besides emptiness,* there will be chaos—and not the kind of chaos that leads to spiritual development."

The imam shoots a glance at Father Carvalho.

"Nature—and God—abhor a vacuum. *Today's culture of emptiness* will be filled with something."

Now his glance turns to Sarah Feld.

"Our souls go shopping, too, Miss Feld, but, as you well know, what they want isn't for sale at the mall. Those who believe otherwise are really saying that spiritual hunger is a weakness which, in the truly 'enlightened' like themselves, has long ago been transformed by 'progress' into a 'mature' self-reliance."

Sarah Feld, whose attention seemed to have been drifting off, turns toward Ashraf Khalifeh, who imperceptibly recoils in anticipation of an attack like the one she made on Father Carvalho.

But instead of attacking, Sarah Feld smiles broadly at the imam and says, "No one in the Akbar Club has been transformed like that, Imam, and is in no danger of being so transformed."

Baghdad to Cairo

I am back in my room at the Palestine Hotel in downtown Baghdad. I had felt apprehensive about voluntarily returning to a location that would soon be within the bounds of the city's own "Ground Zero"—a certain target of bombs. I had consoled myself with the thought that since the hotel was being used by many of the media personalities the American government was counting on to trumpet the attack's inevitable "success," my risk was small. But I am edgy nonetheless.

I had fallen asleep moments after flopping down on the sagging bed, trying to make sense out of what I had experienced that day at Baghdad College. The more I thought about it, the more I was convinced that the Akbar Club's objectives were risible—embarrassingly utopian. Those people couldn't even agree what their message should be. It was one thing to ferret out some long-gone examples of cooperation and even "love" between the three Abrahamic faiths. But how could anyone, even the pope, believe that that kind of cooperation—let alone love—could be fostered today in any significant measure?

We were headed for war. Discussion groups weren't going to save Iraq or tamp down the rage of Islamic extremists.

And yet … the pope was right to try—this was part of his job, and his record on religious conciliation was good.

One thing *is* clear to me. Marthe has gotten under my skin. I seem to be convincing myself that she and I share something that binds us together in ways that do not depend on our actually being together physically.

It wasn't so much that I had finally found my true soul mate. No, it was rather the uneasy sense that *she* had been just waiting for *me* to show up. Beneath her conversation she seemed to whisper: "Now that you are finally here I have the strength I need to complete my task. Now I can go forward."

I bring myself up short. I am not going to surrender to some adolescent mooning about an imaginary connection to someone I like but has never said anything to me suggesting that she might feel something for me.

I decide that what I really feel about Marthe is gratitude for the gift of her sense of peace, her concern, her *presence*.

Although I knew that her completing her task—whatever it was—didn't necessarily involve my help, I nonetheless feel that we would stay together in some way even if we never saw each other again, and that connection would last until one of us explicitly severs it.

Wordlessly, she was appropriating me. It did not occur to me to resist.

Suddenly the Clown is sitting in the room's only chair, tipping it back on two legs against the wall opposite the bed. He looks the same as always.

"That crowd at the college—pretty squirrelly, huh? Imagine trying to do what they say they want to do!

"Oh, well. I guess they can't hurt anyone, and it will keep them out of trouble."

Then all goes black. The bombing has begun. The Clown and I are no longer in my room. We are crouching in a closet of the dilapidated and filthy operating room in a rundown hospital. Through a crack in the door I see two Iraqi doctors, masked and rubber-gloved, bending over the writhing body of a barely conscious adolescent boy. His agonized moans mock the efforts of the anesthesiologist fumbling to affix a pain-obliterating intravenous drip to the boy's neck.

One of the doctors moves slightly to his left and, once again, I can see why the anesthesiologist focuses on the boy's neck: he has no arms. They have been torn from his shoulders by the bomb that less than an hour ago had demolished his family's home.

The boy's mother, her black burqa smeared with dirt and her son's blood, screams curses at the doctors, who labor on, trying to ignore her. In broken English she wails, "They come to kill Saddam, but they ruin my son, our life, our community. Satans! Satans!"

Their hearts pierced by icy shards of guilt and despair, the doctors had glazed, "professional" looks that came nowhere near masking their incomprehension and fear.

The boy's father, his face a numb mask of horror and hate, holds his wife back from the operating table so the doctors can do their work of wrapping another victim in the soiled, infected dressings of a toxic war.

At length, the operation is over, and the boy sleeps. The doctors leave and the boy's parents slump in wicker chairs next to the bed, their faces buried in the grimy sheet on which the boy lay.

I silently creep from the closet, the Clown at my heels, and go into the hallway, where several young members of *MSF* lounge against the wall. Marthe is there. Their faces are frozen in pain and incomprehension, and they fix their gazes on the middle distance in a vain attempt to avoid the horrors that they are seeing and living. My mind flashes back to the Vietnamese child running terrified and naked from her napalmed village.

Across the street from the hospital the Clown and I enter a small church that had held Thérèse's relics. Shrapnel has damaged its roof. Inside are huddled more than one hundred Iraqis, some of whom are Christians—Chaldeans, Roman Catholics, Protestants—and some of whom are Muslims. All are frightened, and many are praying before a statue of Thérèse, which dominates a side altar that is bright with the blaze from dozens of candles.

An old woman warily approaches me and asks if the relics of Thérèse are still in Baghdad. I tell her that the relics are still in the city but are being sheltered from the bombing elsewhere.

She replied, "Her relics may not be here, but she is."

Then the Clown speaks.

"Paul, it's time we got out of here."

The next day I arrive at the French Embassy in the early afternoon. Marthe has given me the name of the attaché who arranged to have the reliquary flown out of the country. Marthe was sure that he could also arrange for a sports utility vehicle to take us out of Baghdad to Jordan, and then on to Cairo. We would reunite there with Father Geli at the Cairo church where Thérèse's devotees were eagerly waiting for the relics.

It will be a dicey operation. The bombing of Baghdad had intensified, and American troops (farcically known as the "coalition forces") would be arriving soon. The runways at the international airport had already been reduced to rubble. Indeed, the skies from Lebanon to Afghanistan are essentially off-limits to all planes that are not American warplanes. We will have to go overland to Cairo, beginning with a drive cross-country to the border with Jordan, over one hundred miles away. We will do this at night—tonight—hoping not to be hijacked by roaming Iraqi members of the Revolutionary Guard or sectarian irregulars, who even now are maneuvering for position and influence in the "new Iraq."

Marthe has pleaded with the French Embassy to be allowed to stay on in Baghdad with her colleagues at *MSF*, but the ambassador herself has insisted that they all evacuate. The ambassador has advised Marthe that she and her *MSF* colleagues can return to Baghdad after the American have secured Iraq, but Marthe is rightly skeptical that that will be possible, given the kinds of security uncertainties that are now the major preoccupation of all nonmilitary foreigners in Iraq.

The ambassador has no jurisdiction over the other members of the Akbar Club who are not French. The only other French member, Sarah Feld, has somehow managed to get the UN's Chief of Mission, an experienced and much-admired Brazilian, and a friend of Father Carvalho, to immediately designate her a UN staffer. This allowed her to stay on to perform emergency services for displaced Iraqi civilians.

Marthe and I sit side by side in the middle seat of the Toyota 4-Runner SUV, staring straight ahead, our passports and exit visas clamped tightly under our arms. It is ten o'clock at night. There is no moon and almost no motorized traffic on the indifferently paved two-lane road.

We are driving very fast through the desolate and dangerous Anbar Province, coming first to the major town of Ramadi. Our headlights show several hundred feet ahead, occasionally illuminating a lone goatherd and his flock huddled at the side of the road, silently praying, I assume, that we not run him over.

Wrapped in green camouflaged canvas in the back, on the floorboard, is a new AK-47 rifle and several full ammunition belts. Next to the rifle is a red Coleman cooler containing bottles of drinking water and some hummus and pita bread for our journey.

Two jerricans of gasoline are strapped to the roof rack.

Our driver, Tarek, is silent, continually checking the murky desert landscape hurtling past on each side. He works for the French Embassy. He is perhaps thirty-eight years old, powerfully built, and taciturn. A loaded pistol is on the seat beside him.

It occurs to me that he might resent being ordered to take on this risky journey for what he might well consider frivolous reasons.

From time to time the thump of bombs, falling on the city we are fleeing, can be felt inside the SUV. Overhead, helicopters—both gunships and troop carriers—shunt past us, on their way to positions on the outskirts of Baghdad.

Marthe and I are silently lost in our thoughts. The evening chill is too sharp for our light jackets, and we instinctively lean close together for warmth. I am thinking again of Jenny. But being with here Marthe makes me less lonely. I'm wondering what she's thinking.

Four hours later, the moon is high. Ahead of us, at the foot of a shallow valley, we can see the border crossing, which is almost encircled with armored vehicles. Armed guards amble around in the semidarkness, their rifles slung muzzle-down on their shoulders. Klieg lights blaze above the forlorn outpost.

About a half mile from the crossing point Tarek slows our SUV to a crawl. He does not want to alarm the guards in case they have not been told to expect us.

Marthe, who has been asleep, opens her eyes and stretches. Her drowsy disorientation, a half-awake vulnerability, excites me. Cautiously, I move a few inches away from her to forestall any awkwardness.

Tarek rolls down his window to speak to the border guard. Then he turns to us to say that our vehicle will be inspected and that we must get out and wait by the side of the road. It will take just a few minutes.

I ask Tarek if the guards had expected us, but he ignores me. I feel a twinge of apprehension. Outwardly, Marthe is serene.

Tarek reaches under the tarp in the back of the SUV and takes out the AK-47 and ammo belts. Then, waving aside our alarmed inquiries, he strides toward a small building fifty yards behind the guard shack, and goes inside.

After about twenty minutes Tarek, without the rifle and ammunition, returns and tells us to get back in the SUV. We are immediately waved through the guard post and into Jordan's desolate eastern desert. It is now four o'clock and the empty sky is becoming a bit lighter—an all-but-imperceptible brightening—as we roar toward Amman, Jordan's capital.

A forlorn highway sign indicates Amman straight ahead and Saudi Arabia left at the next intersection.

I finally risk pressing Tarek on what he did with the rifle and ammo belt. Notably less edgy now that we are out of Iraq, he says that all drivers from Iraq entering Jordan must check their weapons at the border. But since the border police have no room for such an armory, they have asked the local restaurant to help them out. Like renting shoes at the bowling alley, one slides his rifle or handgun into a slot, gets a claim check, and reclaims it on his return leg.

This restaurant's gun-check area was next to the restroom, Tarek volunteers.

Before we have traveled five miles into Jordan, we begin passing first a handful and then dozens of military trucks, hooded headlights dimmed to slender shafts of illumination, headed to Iraq in a reverse exodus. Their loads are covered with tarpaulins, but the tracked vehicles on the flatbed trailers cannot be totally concealed: machine guns and cannons peek out on both sides.

About every ten miles, off to the side of the highway, are small castles that once belonged to Bedouin princes. Tarek says that T. E. Lawrence—"Lawrence of Arabia"—had once holed up in one of them when he was indulging his exotic Orientalist fantasies in the service of the British Empire.

Marthe and I are now wide awake. Both of us had been very anxious about escaping Iraq. Rather than express our fears, we had tried to smother them in forced napping. Now we both wanted to talk, to distract us from the awkwardness of our inadvertent physical intimacy.

"The bombing ..." Marthe's voice trails off.

"The whole thing has an Old Testament taste to it ... as if Yahweh, in His thirst for 'justice' for the attacks on America, has chosen innocent

Iraqi people to suffer ... a plague of bombs and fire. He has handed America His 'terrible swift sword' and said, 'Go get 'em! Smite them! Wreck the lives of innocent people!'"

I turn to look at her. This passion is unexpected.

"This is the kind of 'justice' we criticize in radical Islam! 'He stole? Cut off his hand! She committed adultery? Stone her to death!'

"Christians say 'God is Love,' not 'God is Justice.' For Christ, justice can exist only if it is meted out within the context of His love. Justice can never trump Christ's love, never limit it.

"I don't see Christ's love—or justice—in this bombing. Are we showing Christ's love for his people when we kill them? Are we exercising God's justice when we know that the people we kill are innocent?"

I struggle to find something comforting to say to Marthe. But she has turned her back to me, retreating into herself. I hear her muffled sobs over the whine of our speeding SUV. In a few more minutes she is asleep.

But now the Clown is back, leaning over my right shoulder from the jump seat in the back of the SUV. He hisses, "What about the Hindus, Paul? They're not 'descendants of Father Abraham,' but they're a lot of them around. And they're poor! Isn't that what all this is about? Shouldn't your little club be concerned with them, too?"

"You got another tour in mind for us?" I whisper. I know his style, his *modus operandi*, and I am too tired—and scared—to play his tedious games.

"Another tour—yes—but not *just* for us, bucko, not *just* for us!

"Most of those other folks in your club—that pompous Latino Jesuit, the neurotic Jewish radical, the lovesick African bureaucrat, the Sufi dancer ... I'm not sure they'd really care much about Hindus. They strike me as being very serious about the club's charter—keeping it focused on what they *think* they know.

"But your little French misery minx—here with us—she seems different. She strikes me as an especially sympathetic sort, don't you agree? You wouldn't object to her going along with us, would you?"

Do I catch the hint of a sexual leer in his insinuating tone? I am certain of it. But I also feel something else—a *frisson* of excitement at the prospect of Marthe's being with me on the next leg of the Clown's perpetual circus tour.

"Of course, it would all be like a dream to her—just as it was with you when we first met ... before we got so well acquainted, you might say."

I'm hooked but try to hide it.

"What do you have in mind?" I ask, too eagerly.

"Before we get to Amman, a quick trip to India—to Varanasi, the white-hot center of Hindu worship. Maybe you both can pick up some pointers there that just might make your colleagues at the Akbar Club think you know something they don't."

We're off.

Tent No. 6: Varanasi
The Ever-Turning Wheel of Life Churns a Murky River!

It's the eve of the festival of Dalachat. Tomorrow at dawn, mothers will carry oil lamps to the Ganges River and pray to the Lord Sun for their sons' long lives.

It is dusk. We are in a van driven by the guide, Siddarth. The Clown is beside him in the front seat, but, as usual for these fantasy tours, only I can see and hear him. Marthe and I are in the back seat. She is wearing a sari.

We drive over a short bridge and see women below, swathed in bright saris. As if rehearsing for tomorrow's ritual, they launch their little lamps, set in grass holders, onto the narrow river.

Darkness is fast approaching as we proceed downtown into a maelstrom of surging humanity, each person contending for space with his rickshaw, bike, cart, or tuk-tuk. The chaotic street is choking in dust and fumes, barely lit by the snapping, buzzing neon lights from curbside shops and stalls. I feel utterly trapped and immobile, a sense of alarm creeping over me. I can't recall such a claustrophobic injection of abject fear. Marthe shows no outward sign of distress. She stares out the window, her features a mask of rapt wonderment.

Finally, at about nine o'clock, we break free and retreat to the local Oberoi Hotel, a musty and second-rate place, leave a wake-up call for five the next morning, and retire to our separate rooms. Tomorrow we will go to the Ganges for the festival.

Up before first light, we have a quick breakfast, and, now joined noise-lessly (and, for Marthe, invisibly) by the Clown, depart for the ghats—the mile-long strip of concrete steps sloping steeply to the bathing and cremation terraces along the west bank of the river a hundred yards below. It is the final day of the festival, and Siddarth says that mothers will bring their oil lamps to the river to greet Lord Sun when he rises precisely at six twenty. Families and friends will pour milk onto the lamps, which the mothers will hold in grass baskets as they stand hip deep in the water and turn in circles.

I mutter something about the ceremony resembling a Sufi *sema*. Siddarth, a Buddhist, looks at me quizzically. The Clown laughs, "I don't think he knows what you're talking about, my friend!" Marthe nods her agreement with me.

We drive through narrow, dung-strewn alleys, still drowsy in the dim half-light of dawn, twisting interminably and ending up at the top of a ghat, the Ganges far below us.

We meet our teenage "boatman" (rower) and clamber down to his ten-foot-long dory. In the bilges four or five oil lamps, some still lit, float in the muck. We buy two lamps from a young girl, who lights them for us with a long taper and clamber aboard the dory. Our rower inserts the bamboo oars into the cloth oar locks.

Marthe wordlessly breathes a zephyr of intimacy toward me.

We push off and join the parade of other spectator boats, some with up to twenty-five passengers, and head downriver toward the major ghats, keeping about one hundred fifty yards offshore.

A riotous scene. The ghats and concrete stairs are packed with excited Indians of all ages. Most are here for the festival, but some, mostly older men, are clearly here only to perform their daily ablutions. The women are in a dazzling array of saris, standing in the river and splashing the water on their faces while friends hold their oil lamps.

Firecrackers explode, echoing sharply against the ghats. Flags and streamers flutter in the cool morning breeze.

As daybreak approaches, the hubbub grows louder. Then, suddenly, a sliver of sun peeks over the misty horizon to the east, and a thunderous roar goes up. Sheer joy. The fireworks explosions intensify and high up in the ghats, on a stone platform, a brass band plays raucous, eerie tunes. Women holding grass trays of oil laps begin to turn in circles—their faces in a trance. Bystanders, mostly men, pour milk onto the lamps, and onto the other celebrants pressing close.

We see two young Western women, clad in saris and submerged to the waist, gaze toward the rising sun, hands to foreheads in the traditional *namaste* position. After several minutes of contemplation they turn and begin to walk back up the submerged portion of the ghat steps, gradually emerging onto dry steps.

Marthe stares at them from our dory, transfixed. Just as they reach the dry steps, Marthe shouts, "Wait for me!" She then eases herself over the side of the boat and disappears beneath the greasy surface of the river.

Instantly, a loud, approving roar erupts from the Indian celebrants watching from the bank. Startled, the two Western women turn around just as Marthe surfaces and begins dog-paddling toward them on the bank, her soggy sari trailing behind her.

As Marthe climbs onto the dry steps, gathering her sari about her, the two young women bend down to steady her. They exchange brief, animated words that I cannot hear as they wring their saris. Then they embrace like schoolgirls and, holding hands, turn in a circle, ring-around-the-rosy style, laughing with delight. The onlookers cheer again, even louder than before.

Our boatman rows us toward them, but by the time we get there, the two women are halfway up the ghat steps, followed by at least fifty of their new fans. Marthe, looking unapologetic, steps back into the dory to the cheers of perhaps twenty bystanders, and we head wordlessly back upriver toward our boarding point.

As we slowly slide upstream we see holy men (*saddhus*) high up in the ghats, sitting cross-legged in niches carved into the stone walls, lost in mystical prayer.

Further along we see the ghats where cremations occur. A large brick building with two tall smokestacks is for the "commercial" cremations that only wealthy families can afford. I think fleetingly of Sarah Feld—and Auschwitz—but with the vital difference that these are religious, not genocidal, cremations.

Next to the building, on a narrow platform, sits a thirty-foot stack of firewood. Off to the side are the areas where open-air cremations of the poor occur. Sweepers with brooms and rakes, clad only in loin cloths, groom the smoking coals.

The spectator boats jostle for position—cameras click, tape rolls. Drops of river water strike my arm. I think typhoid.

After about thirty minutes, we arrive at our starting point, climb the ghat, and retrace our steps, dodging hawkers, and head toward the van, which we had parked on a side street.

I try to assimilate what I had just witnessed on the holy river. The poverty among the celebrants and their families was just as dire as any I had seen in Africa, Russia, or Southeast Asia. If anything, the crush of penniless humanity was denser here than there. But whereas the poor of those other regions seemed to survive by donning the armor of resignation and hospitality—and, in Russia, something close to despair—here the poor rely on vivid ceremony and an acceptance of the physical side of life—of poverty out in the open—that is almost frightening to Western eyes and sensibilities: a threatening fusion of the physical and the spiritual.

Could these alien characteristics be incorporated into the Akbar Club's discussions? I am doubtful. But then I remember that, after all, Akbar was in some sense an Indian. How did *he* incorporate Hinduism into his spiritual synthesis?

It is all too much.

The Clown looks pleased.

We take Amman's beltway and skirt the central city—where rush-hour traffic, swollen by thousands of recently arrived Iraqis refugees, is streaming—and head northwest toward the Jordan Valley village of Faysaliyah, where Mount Nebo, almost three thousand feet above sea level, is located. We snake our way up the access road to the summit and are met by two Franciscan friars, who are expecting us. Franciscans maintain the renovated fourth-century church and monastery and regulate the nonstop flow of tour buses and cars that visit daily.

Although there are no overnight facilities for pilgrims at Mount Nebo, the Franciscans have agreed to let us stay in the monastery, tucked out of sight behind the small restored church. At dawn, we will continue our odyssey south to Jordan's Red Sea port of Aqaba. From there we will board a speedboat and head southwest overnight to the Sinai trekker village of Dahab. Then we will drive across the Sinai and under the Suez Canal to Cairo, where we will rejoin Father Geli and the relics.

I had to admire the efficiency—and *élan*—of the French ambassador in Baghdad, who had made these complex arrangements on very short notice.

Our hosts, the two friars, lead us up the stone pathway to the summit and direct our eyes to the west. In the foreground is the Dead Sea, and in the bright morning light we see Jerusalem in the distance, just as Moses did from this, his closest approach to the Promised Land. Between the Dead Sea and Jerusalem is Jericho, in the West Bank. Marthe inquires whether it's possible to see Mount Carmel, on the Mediterranean coast, where the Carmelites, St. Thérèse's order, was founded.

"No," says our host, "that's too far away ... But I can feel the Carmelite spirit here. Through you it is here. *You* have brought Mount Carmel here!"

At dawn we drive slowly back down the access road and bear left past the highway leading to the Queen Alia International Airport and ease onto the main highway heading south to Petra and our destination, Aqaba, at the northern tip of the Gulf of Aqaba, which flows into the Red Sea.

Two hours later we pass the turnoffs to Petra, on the right, and Wadi Rum, on the left. Petra is the site of the ancient Nabatean civilization, which carved exquisite buildings from the local stone. Today it is mostly known as the site where the film *The Raiders of the Lost Ark* was shot.

Wadi Rum is the center of the jagged red-rock region of southern Jordan that reminds me of northern Arizona. Bedouin tribesmen and their camels, sheep, and goats still largely inhabit this part of the country.

As we approach Aqaba, we pass long lines of dilapidated trucks, their cargos concealed and sheathed beneath tattered tarpaulins. They are coming from Aqaba, Jordan's only seaport, and are transporting the arms and supplies to the American invaders, whose contracted ships have brought them here. They labor up the rocky and winding road toward Amman and the eastern desert road to Iraq, which we had traversed yesterday.

Another hour passes—it is now eight thirty—and we begin our winding descent to Aqaba. To our right, in the foreground, the waterfront is lined with five-star hotels along a narrow beach. In the distance is the Israeli town of Eilat, hovering like a nervous chaperone in a neighborhood of unruly teenagers. To our left, in a grand arc, is, first the commercial port, and, some two miles beyond, the border with Saudi Arabia.

The commercial port is jammed with cargo vessels of diverse provenance, as shown by the flags they fly. Panamanian- and Liberian-registered ships predominate, of course, but the Marshall Islands, Palau, Micronesia, and other such sunny and forlorn havens are also represented. The one common characteristic is the countries' ties to, and dependence upon, the United States.

At the city's outskirts we encounter an unexpected security roadblock. Tarek instructs us to remain silent and deals with the two Jordanian army guards himself. There is a moment of anxiety as the guards retire to their hut to consider whether to allow us to pass. One of them makes a phone call. Marthe instinctively presses closer to me.

At length the guards reemerge and wave us through. We bear left and head to the commercial port along the corniche. After passing the port's entrance we turn into the driveway of the Royal Jordanian Dive Shop, whose wooden pier extends fifty yards into the gulf. There are no divers in evidence—no doubt the maritime traffic jam and the heightened security have discouraged—perhaps even proscribed—tourism of any kind for the duration.

A fifteen-foot speedboat, looking very much like an old wood-sided Chris-Craft, is tied up at the end of the dock, near the diving platform. Two Jordanian men emerge from the dive shack near where we have parked the SUV, and Tarek goes over to meet them.

It occurs to me that it was these men whom the security guard at the edge of town had phoned.

After a very short conversation, Tarek returns to the SUV, and the two men go back to the dive shack. Tarek says that Marthe and I will take the speedboat to Dahab, where we will be met by another guide-driver to take us the rest of the way to Cairo. Tarek gently advises us to take advantage of the dive shack's toilet before boarding the speedboat, whose "head," he says, is serviceable but not very private.

One of the men from the dive shack joins us at the SUV and hands me a covered wicker basket containing food and water for our overnight run to Dahab. Tarek bids us a brusque farewell, gets back into the SUV, and drives off. His manner suggests to me that he intends to drive nonstop back to Baghdad.

Our skipper gingerly eases the speedboat around and past the dozen or so cargo ships waiting at anchor for a berth to unload. Far above us, leaning over the rails of each ship, sharpshooters and lookouts warily watch us. For the first time since leaving Baghdad I feel truly afraid. I am keenly aware that not long ago an American warship was attacked in Aden's harbor by a boat smaller than ours. Today, no self-respecting guard would hesitate to shoot us instantly if he had the slightest suspicion that we were dangerous.

In thirty minutes we clear the clogged harbor and head at speed south through the Gulf of Aqaba toward the open sea. The bow of our boat slaps through the choppy waters, and Marthe and I wordlessly resign ourselves to an uncomfortable night. I think of Douglas MacArthur's World War II dash from Corregidor in the Philippines to safety, in Australia. Dahab is our Australia.

Dusk is brief, and the sun sets quickly behind the stark hills and mountains of the Sinai. We pick at our "picnic" dinner—hummus, pita, olives, and peppers—and wrap ourselves in blankets and restlessly catnap for the rest of the night.

In no time, it seems, it is light. I peer past the bow of our boat to the forbidding shoreline, which, even at five thirty in the morning, bounces on the thermals like a trampoline. The sun—and temperature—are rising fast, and I can barely make out the signs of the quickening bustle around Dahab's main pier.

Beyond the beach, still cloaked in their bluish nighttime haze, I can see the indistinct outlines of the Sinai's rocky peaks, devoid of all vegetation and almost defying the traveler to set foot on them.

We step ashore into a sleepy, scruffy fishing-and-diving village whose inhabitants, overwhelmingly young Europeans, are just beginning to rouse themselves from what, judging from their vacant looks and the ambient aroma, must have been a pot-besotted night.

Strung like beads along the beach side of the rutted shoreline road are scruffy lanais that resemble David Roberts's prints of long-gone Middle Eastern harems. Open on all four sides, they are stuffed with thick pillows and low-slung cots. Their overhead shelters of dull-colored carpets and cloths sag from supporting poles.

Overall, a vibe of the mild decadence that so inspired Flaubert several generations ago, before he returned to Normandy to write *Madam Bovary*. I mention this thought to Marthe. She appears amused. I briefly fantasize about what it might be like to be here with her under other circumstances.

She catches me staring at her and smiles.

Our speedboat skipper supervises our transfer to our new SUV, whose driver, a thirtysomething Egyptian, he had phoned from the boat. Marthe and I have a quick breakfast of coffee and sweet rolls in a nearby café, and within an hour of our arrival are on our way west to the Nile River and, beyond that, Cairo.

At midday we arrive at St. Catherine's, the ancient Orthodox monastery at the base of Mount Sinai. Our driver is talking on his cell phone with someone as we pull into a parking lot jammed with tour buses from Cairo. Middle-aged and elderly tourists—almost all of them, it appears, from Europe—straggle toward the reception area, clutching their bottles of water. Some of the younger ones clamber up the smooth face of the rocky hill facing the monastery and train their binoculars on the peak of the mountain, where Moses is said to have received the Ten Commandments from Yahweh.

Here and there, oblivious to the bustle, black-robed monks hurry along to their devotions and chores, lost in their own thoughts. More watchful are the ubiquitous police in their blue uniforms, strolling in pairs around the parking area, their rifles casually slung over their shoulders.

Our driver advises Marthe and me to take advantage of this rest stop while he waits for one of the on-duty monks to bring us a box lunch from the tourist cafeteria. It is clear that we won't be spending much time here.

To our left the sun is setting quickly as we drive north along the Sinai highway. In under an hour we pass under the Suez Canal and head south for Cairo.

Our driver has been on his cell phone for over an hour.

Then I notice it: the smell of the Nile after the heat of the day has waned. I know this smell. I had known it on the Amazon, the Mekong in Laos, the Chao Phaya in Thailand. It is a smell one doesn't encounter on western rivers—on the Seine, Thames, Hudson, or even the Mississippi. It is the smell of riverine poverty: pungent, acrid, yet somehow nostalgic and oddly comforting.

And I knew from experience that you taste it before you actually smell it—a musky mixture of dust, vegetation, and smoky haze that settles in a thin veneer over the water—a poor-world smell, but the smell of life, not death.

The last feluccas of the day tack lazily back and forth across the river, and as they meander, seemingly without destination, they trail delicate wakes, like fingers being lightly drawn over a dusty piano in a long-shuttered parlor.

Along the far bank of the river, as if guarding the fields from floods, are long columns of palm trees, sagging sentinels bent by the heat. Behind them, extending away from the river toward the western horizon, hundreds of small plots of vegetables, wheat, and sugar cane, like quilts drying on the ground.

In a way that, for me, is totally uncharacteristic, I share my reverie with Marthe. She takes my hand and says, "Yes, there's something here alright. Even Flaubert felt it!"

She slowly withdraws her hand.

Our SUV pulls into the curved driveway of the Zamalek Marriott Hotel, on the east bank of the Nile, a building that was built for the French Empress Eugenie, consort of Napoleon III, as a place she could stay while attending the ceremonies attending the opening of the Suez Canal in 1869. Two gigantic and mustachioed doormen, dressed in long red tunics and white turbans, immediately bear down on us from beneath the awning over the hotel's main entrance. Ignoring the pleas of other arriving guests in search of help with their luggage, one of the doormen swings our car door open and greets us with a blast of heartiness that for some reason makes me immediately suspicious.

Clearly, we are expected.

Leaving our driver with the vehicle, Marthe and I walk into the hotel and are ushered to the head of the check-in queue, which contains about thirty people just off a tour bus.

We endure an awkward moment when the desk clerk assumes we wish to share a room. He briskly sorts it out and hands us our passkeys.

The hotel manager steps toward us from behind the desk, from which, I had noticed, he has been observing us checking in. Two stern-faced men who appear to be in their early sixties accompany him. One is in formal business dress and the other appears to be an Egyptian cleric.

The manager introduces himself and his friends to us as the French ambassador to Egypt and the Vatican's ambassador (the papal nuncio). The Frenchman offers his calling card to me, ignoring Marthe, and

announces that the nuncio has asked him to take responsibility for the reliquary, which is already being attended by Father Geli at St. Tereza
Church in the sprawling Shobra district, three miles away on the other
side of the Nile. The nuncio silently nods his confirmation and hands me
his own calling card.

The French ambassador then gives me a sealed letter and indicates that
I should read it now. It's a handwritten note from Father Geli welcoming
me to Cairo and informing us that the relics will be on display at the
church for one week, beginning at nine o'clock tomorrow evening. I am to
meet him there tomorrow evening. I can bring Marthe if I insist.

I look up from the note and thank everyone for their assistance. The
two diplomats bid us stiff farewells and depart.

Marthe and I are greatly relieved to have accomplished our mission. We
agree to meet in two hours' time in the hotel's garden for dinner and (at
least for me) a drink, and go to our rooms.

The garden promenade is two hundred yards from end to end and bor-
dered by cushioned armchairs and round, wrought iron tables, a vast
open-air restaurant buzzing with life. Parents call after their fleeing children, modish young people murmur into cell phones, and their elders,
slumped deep in their chairs, survey the scene with vague disapproval
through rheumy eyes.

Women encased from head to toe in black burquas stare straight ahead
through eye slits, their fierce glances alive with provocative invitations that
their secular sisters could only envy.

Fez-topped men, placidly sucking on their *shisha* bubble pipes at
crowded tables, glower at passersby like toads on their lily pads waiting for
unwary insects.

I thread my way through the humming crush, careful to avoid the scur-
rying waiters and careening teenagers on skateboards.

As I near the far end on the promenade I note a table of middle-aged
American men whom I recognize from the restaurant in Baghdad's Palestine Hotel. They are relaxed and wear shorts and bright polo shirts and
suck on *shishas*. I recognize them as intelligence agents, here to escape
Baghdad's bombing—agents who will return to Baghdad when it is safer.

I am quite certain that one of them recognizes me. I remember speaking
to him briefly in one of the churches where the relics had been. He had

been the only other Westerner in the church, and we had talked briefly about Thérèse, with whose story he seemed quite familiar.

I had wondered at the time if Shadow Peirce had asked him to keep an eye on me.

I look away, perhaps a little too quickly. Five seconds later the touch on my sleeve and faux-hearty "Paul!" confirm my suspicions.

"I work with Shadow Peirce. You and I chatted briefly in Baghdad … in a church.

"I'm glad you and Marthe made it out of Iraq OK. It's going to get ugly there."

C'est Sufis

The phone next to my bed is ringing, but I'm still trying to get my bearings. I check my alarm clock and see that it is five thirty in the afternoon. My head aches.

I look around the room and remember that I am in Cairo, at the Marriott in Zamalek. Marthe and I have been in Cairo for twenty-four hours, and I have spent most of them sleeping. I pick up the ringing phone.

It is Marthe. She reminds me that Father Geli wants us at St. Tereza Church at nine o'clock for the official start of the relics' visit.

She then adds that before going to the church she wants to see the weekly performance of the "whirling dervishes" at the Ghuriyya Cultural Centre, next to the Khan el-Khalili market and Al-Azhar University, Sunni Islam's most prominent center of learning. She says that she knows that if she goes to the performance she'll be late arriving at the church, but she's sure that Father Geli can be mollified—"he'll be too busy to even notice."

She asks me to accompany her, and I eagerly accept, jumping at the chance to be alone again with her, not having to share her attention—her *presence*—with others. Almost as an afterthought she adds that she knows the leader of the musical group that will be accompanying the dancers and wants me to meet him.

We have a quick dinner on the promenade and leave for the Cultural Centre.

Our wheezing taxi climbs onto one of the flyovers crisscrossing Cairo's raucous core, high above the train station and Jesuit high school where the French paleontologist and mystic Teilhard de Chardin had his first teaching job. We look down on garishly lit mosques, seedy neighborhood markets, and desolate housing projects. People stir listlessly in the early evening air, thick with a hazy gauze of pollution. They are like small fish swimming in the haze. Old men hunched over in wooden chairs in dark doorways, sucking on their bubble pipes. Teenagers in gaudy colors circling restlessly, searching for something—anything—to dispel the enervating boredom—searching for someone on whom to bestow their longing.

Marthe's serene introspection is unaffected by the sweltering taxi and the stifling atmosphere.

As we approach the entrance to the market through the honking cars and surging pedestrians, we see the massive el-Azhar Mosque, whose stiletto minarets thrust skyward like phosphorous sparklers from a stone birthday cake. Marthe has the driver drop us a block from the Cultural Centre, and we join the throng of people hurrying to the performance.

Inside, perhaps two hundred people crowd around the floor where the dancers will perform, their faces bright with anticipation. We can find no vacant seats close to the floor, so retreat to the wall forty feet back, where standees struggle to keep from being pushed even further away by other latecomers.

Incredibly, I think for an instant that I see Shadow Peirce against the wall, some forty feet away. But when I refocus, he has disappeared. I am relieved. I have not seen him since my fantasy trip to Central Asia, and I don't want him pressing me again about returning to Baghdad.

In fact, I don't ever want to see him again.

Presently, the musicians—four of them—weave their way down the crowded aisle toward the dance floor. They will pass close to where Marthe and I are standing. I notice that they are Westerners, not Egyptians, and that their dress would not have been out of place onstage at Carnegie Hall: black shoes, tuxedos, and bow ties, not the Arabic dress of the audience or the ceremonial dress of the eight waiting dancers, who are themselves now coming onto the floor.

The musicians' instruments await them just off the dance floor: a piano, a cello, a clarinet, and something I had not seen before—a bizarre contraption that looks part piano and part zither, a small keyboard surmounted by a rectangular metal frame which is strung with steel strings.

As they draw even to Marthe and me, one of the musicians—the one who appears by his age and demeanor to be the leader—spots Marthe and stops in his tracks. While his companions stand by, this round-faced gentleman smacks his broad forehead with his palm in surprise, pushes his wispy white hair away from his horn-rimmed glasses, and embraces Marthe in heartfelt greeting.

After an exchange of pleasantries that I only half hear, Marthe turns to me and introduces him as Maestro Thierry Blum, the foremost contemporary interpreter of the celebrated modernist composer Olivier Messiaen. He clasps my outstretched hand in both of his and says he hopes I will enjoy the performance.

Marthe says that "Maestro" will play the strange instrument tonight. Before I can ask what it is, Mr. Blum says in a shy voice, "It's an *ondes-martenot*. I'm guessing you have never heard it before—I think you'll like it."

The musicians walk onto the dance floor and take up their instruments.

Marthe turns to me and says that they will be performing Blum's own composition based on Messiaen's *Quartet for the End of Time*, which she describes as a "dissonant and haunting contemplation of *The Revelation of St. John*." She adds, almost as an afterthought, that Messiaen had written the piece while a prisoner of the German army in Poland in the frigid winter of 1941, and that he and three other prisoner-musicians had first performed it for their fellow inmates using instruments that, inexplicably, had been supplied by their guards.

Marthe has a faraway look on her face now, as if she is meditating on what she has just told me.

Before I can assimilate this latest dip into her mysterious depths, Maestro Blum and his colleagues begin to play. The clarinet and the piano launch into a contrapuntal recitative "conversation" of birdsong call-and-response, which instantly dissolves the audience's restiveness.

The dancers—all of them male—slowly begin to sway. They are wrapped in floor-length black cloaks symbolizing mortality and life's worldly cares and pleasures. On their heads are elongated white felt fezzes, which cover their ears and resemble inverted flowerpots. Staring straight ahead they glide single file around the dance floor three times, sinking ever deeper into a meditative trance. The short first movement is suddenly over.

The second movement begins with the clarinet and piano dueling in a sour clash of sound. The birds are angry. Then Blum begins to play the *ondes-martenot*. With his left hand he strikes minor chords. With his right hand he runs a steel bar over the steel strings that are strung to the metal frame above the keyboard. The effect is whiney and ethereal, not unlike the soundtrack of a science-fiction movie from the 1960s.

The otherworldly mood is intensified by the motion of the dancers, who by now have arranged themselves around the perimeter of the floor, shedding their black cloaks, and revealing the pure white, full skirts that, as they spin, flow up and around them in a frenzied choreography of spiritual transport. Marthe whispers that the white skirts are meant to resemble shrouds.

The dancers start by slowly twirling in time to the music. Their eyes are open but unfocused. For five or six minutes they twirl around and around, their spins straining toward a gathering crescendo, the music spurring them on to another plane of consciousness.

The third movement begins as a prolonged and dreamy woodwind reverie, punctuated by dovelike warbling. As it gains pace, two new figures, females, appear on the floor. I turn to my right to point them out to Marthe, but she is not beside me. When I turn back to the floor I recognize the new dancers: Marthe herself ... and Sarah Feld! They have formed their own unit in the center of the male dancers and are slowly moving among them, interweaving with them in an ethereal round. For several minutes they slowly move, like the male dancers, lost in their own world.

As the movements follow one another, the *ondes-martenot* and piano regain the musical initiative and the pace becomes ever more frenzied. Marthe and Sarah are spinning in a tight Dionysian duo of their own, oblivious to all around them. They spin clockwise as individuals and the circle they have formed slowly turns clockwise as well.

Almost imperceptibly the male dancers, still spinning, surround Marthe and Sarah in a circle that slowly turns counterclockwise.

Then, some members of the audience—mostly very poor, judging from their dress—leave their seats, step onto the floor, and start to twirl. They gradually array themselves into a third, outer circle, which turns clockwise.

I feel that I am watching an ancient country courting dance, except that the intensity of the dancers is the opposite of flirtatious. They have moved beyond the physical to the ethereal.

The music slowly winds down, in both tempo and volume, and the dancers and the audience begin to drift away. Marthe and Sarah have vanished. It is almost eight o'clock, and after waiting for several minutes, I leave the hall, hurt at Marthe's having deserted me without an explanation. And when did Sarah arrive in Cairo? I take a taxi back to the hotel.

When I ask for my room key at the front desk the clerk hands me a note in an envelope. It is a note from Marthe.

Dear Paul,

I'm sorry I left you so suddenly! I remembered that I had promised some friends I would meet them early at St. Tereza's for the Mass marking Thérèse's feast day today. I had to go directly to the church from the sema. Sarah will come to the church, too but had to return to the hotel first. I asked her to have the concierge give you this note. I hope to see you there, too! The concierge will tell you how to get there on the metro. Please be at the church by 9:30.

Forgive me! I promise never to abandon you like this again!
Marthe

I feel ill and slump down heavily into a nearby sofa.

At nine o'clock, on Tahrir Square near the Egyptian Museum in central Cairo, I board the *metro* for Shobra, three stops away. The rush hour is long over, but the train is packed. Many of the passengers, among them entire families, carry furled banners and posters. Later, when they are unfurled, I see that they bear the image of St. Thérèse.

The train stops first at the Sadat and Mubarak stations, but almost no one gets off. At the Shobra station, officially named "St. Tereza," the train empties and the passengers pour from the station exit, unroll their banners, and begin to march the three long blocks to the church, singing as they go. I fall in with a family.

A block from the church, we join the restless queue waiting to view the relics, which are in the reliquary just outside the wrought iron fence that encloses the church grounds.

Priests and nuns reciting prayers from small breviaries ring the platform supporting the reliquary. Mixing with them are bearded Muslim clerics in skullcaps, who read aloud from the Koran.

I look around for Father Geli but do not see him.

Muslim men and women, some in colorful scarves and some in black burquas, mill about singing. The women's keening ululations are an eerie counterpoint to the traditional hymns to Mary sung by Christian worshipers.

A small space around the platform has been cleared so that the faithful may draw close, ten at a time. Clouds of pungent incense billow from censers, which acolytes swing in great arcs. Emotions run high—like those of the Iraqi faithful whom I had recently seen.

The light has faded in the early spring evening. As I inch my way toward the platform I notice the church's exterior, which is illuminated by recessed lights. A Romanesque structure whose façade is studded with roses hewn from pink stone, its overall effect owes more to the religious sensibilities of Byzantium than those of Europe.

The church is one hundred fifty years old. A brass marker on the wrought iron fence says that in 1950, twenty-three years after her canonization, it had been renamed for St. Thérèse at the insistence of her Egyptian devotees. It is plain that the intervening years has only intensified the ardor of those devotees, an ardor that boils here at a level like that at the Marian shrine at Lourdes, in France.

After a quick glance at the relics I make my way toward the church. It stands at the foot of a downward-sloping, oval driveway that is lined with bushes and flowering plants. Urban grime is gradually but inexorably enshrouding it.

As I approach the main door I notice small, white, square plaques lining the portico from floor to ceiling, each one—in Arabic, Latin, English, or French—thanking Thérèse for the birth of a healthy child, recovery from an illness, success of a venture, or some other blessing.

In a large glass case on the portico's right side are several photographs of a young Thérèse, a girl, and a dying nun. A knot of people stares at them in prayerful silence.

I enter the church and am struck by the contrast between its chaotic mélange of ecclesiastical styles and Thérèse's celebrated simplicity.

Rainbow stonework, reflecting Egypt's Coptic heritage, clashes with Renaissance touches like the Bernini-style columns supporting the canopy over the altar, itself a smaller version of the altar of St. Peter's Basilica, in Rome.

The interior walls are a pastiche of dingy stone, some painted in garish colors, suggesting a forlorn attempt to revive a faded Victorian parlor through the random daubing of bright hues.

Florescent-lighted icons of Mary, Joseph, and other saints top baroque pulpits and supporting columns, each with the oval face of Coptic iconography.

High above the main altar, against the rear wall, is the most jarring touch of all: a round painting of St. Thérèse in her brown and sand colored Carmelite habit, cradling the traditional bouquet of roses, and ringed by twenty large, naked, orange, carnival-style light bulbs, several of which have gone dark. Appropriate for a circus, I think.

I briefly consider what symbolism this harsh clash of the celestial and the vulgar might contain—modern man's spiritual lights going out along with his faith, perhaps?—but quickly give up and look away.

I find a seat midway up the center aisle, on the right. Within minutes I have been nudged from my position on the aisle to the middle of the pew, jostled by people on either side.

Presently the platform and reliquary are wheeled into the church and placed in the nave, near my pew.

A small bell tinkles and suddenly the altar is crowded with four priests and perhaps fifteen male servers. Some of the servers are very young, perhaps ten years old, and others are in their twenties or thirties. All wear pure white surplices emblazoned with crosses of bright red silk.

The presiding priest has a beard and forbidding demeanor that suggests not so much devotion as stern discipline, reinforcing an atmosphere very much at odds with St. Thérèse's legendary accessibility. He motions the servers to their respective stations with a proprietary yet intimate brusqueness that made me uncomfortably recall Flaubert's description of his dalliances with local boys in Cairo's saunas.

Mass proceeds, and when it is time for the homily, the presiding priest fairly spits it out in Arabic, which, of course, I cannot fully understand. However, with my rudimentary knowledge of the language, I make out a perfunctory reprise of St. Thérèse's life and her current position as the object of worldwide veneration. The solemnity of the distribution of hosts is marred by a frantic crush of communicants, who storm the altar rail as if this were their one chance to receive the last rites.

Just before Mass ends, several burly men wheel the reliquary toward the altar and carry it down the broad flight of steps that lead to the small crypt below. People immediately spill from the pews, but instead of leaving the church, they again storm the altar and push their way down the stairs to the crypt.

I had not planned on joining them but soon see that I have no other choice. I cannot leave the church in any event, so dense is the crowd behind me. I soon find myself the tallest person in the round, low-ceilinged crypt, softly lit by candles at its perimeter. The walls are lined with the same kind of grayish white commemorative tiles that adorn the church's portico.

In the center of the crypt stands the reliquary, next to a glass-enclosed box that resembles a large jewelry display case. Inside the box is a full-length statue of a reclining Thérèse, in her habit. She is tilted to her right side, lips slightly parted, eyes closed. Her right hand, palm up and loosely cradling a brown-beaded rosary, hangs open fingered at her side. Pressing their palms to the glass, the devotees moan their tearful prayers and petitions.

The statue's facial expression is a sensuous blend of languid transport and submissive femininity that reminds me of Bernini's celebrated sculpture of St. Teresa of Avila, which I had once seen in a Carmelite church near Rome's central train station. That masterpiece embodied both the corporeal and spiritual aspects of what some call the Eternal Feminine. But it seemed to go beyond the simple linkage of carnality and spirituality. It suffused the carnal *into* the spiritual to create a higher spirituality—a spirituality that still lures man to woman, but also takes him on to God.

My reverie is abruptly doused in a dizzying blast of cloying incense and the naked display of spiritual neediness. My head is light, and my knees buckle. I wheel around, push my way back through the oncoming crowd, and struggle up the steps, bent on escaping into the cool evening.

As I shuffle toward the church's main entrance, out of the corner of my eye I catch a glimpse of a familiar face in a pew against the far right wall, nearly obscured in the interior's half-light: Ashraf Khalifeh, from the Akbar Club.

He hails me over. I join him, repressing my astonishment at seeing him there. I am annoyed to be plunged once again into the twilit world I thought I had left in Baghdad.

Ashraf Khalifeh greets me, diffident as ever. He doesn't say how he happens to be here in this church, in Cairo. Perhaps he had traveled from Baghdad with Sarah Feld.

"I am concerned about Marthe," he says. "We were dancing at a *sema* earlier this evening. Miss Feld was there, too. Marthe and I made plans to come here together, but at the last minute she said she would be late because she had an appointment to see someone first.

"She doesn't know Cairo very well ... she missed Mass. I'm worried about her."

I had not recognized Khalifeh among the dancers at the *sema*.

"I wouldn't be too concerned, Imam," I said, not very convincingly. "She left me a note that said she would be here with Sarah Feld. I'm sure she was delayed and just couldn't make it."

I mutter good-bye and head for the church door. Disorientation is clamping its firm grip on my mind.

It was then that I hear a familiar voice behind me. Marthe's voice? I can't quite make out her words, but I think I hear faint strains of the music from the Sufi dance, the *sema*. I stop in my tracks and slowly turn around. Marthe isn't there. No one I know is near me.

My eyes drift to the picture above the altar. The grotesque light bulbs are now dark, and I can just barely see St. Thérèse's picture. Marthe's voice seemed to come from there, but I'm not sure.

On Thérèse's right is the Clown. He is looking at her, a stunned expression on the side of his painted face that I could see.

Then both slowly begin to turn. I start to look away, but as I do so I notice that the picture has begun to pulsate, fading away and then gradu-

ally coming back into focus. The Clown and Thérèse are twirling fever-
ishly now.

When the picture is fully clear again, the Clown is gone. My image has
replaced his, and alongside me, fading in and out of the picture, are people
the Clown and I had met in circuses all over the world: the running kids in
The Gambia ... the newspaper stuffer in Dorothy Day's mission in New
York ... a bent old man in Zagorsk ... the freezing woman on Arbat Street
... the cricket-eating crone in Luang Prabang ... the proud but desperate
museum guide in Phnom Penh ... the young Hindu girl selling floating
lamps by the Ganges ... the quietly despairing mothers in the Azerbaijani
refugee camp. We are all twirling in a ragged version of the Sufi *sema*.

Then the garish lights surrounding the picture flicker to life—their
orange glow illuminating the entrance of yet another worn circus tent.
Over the main entrance a sign reads:

Welcome to Paradise, Verse 21! The Eternal Saturnal Sema!

Then my image fades, and the Clown's returns.

I hear the voice again.

"Good evening, Paul!"

Thérèse's picture seems to be speaking.

"Isn't this great? I convinced this good clown and his friends to join us
here this evening. I'm glad you're here, too."

Thérèse's lips don't move, but in every other respect, her picture is
speaking to me. Her voice is very like Marthe's.

"Paul, this clown knows the secret of the poor!"

I seize the panel of the nearest pew for support. After a long pause I find
my voice.

"But ... I *still* have no idea what their secret is!"

The Clown erupts.

"Oh, *please*, Paul! Must we draw you a picture? Why are you even here
in this place? There is no mystery! It's all quite clear!

"Did you see Marthe tonight at the *sema*? She abandoned herself to the
spirit. *You* feel the pull of that abandonment ... accept it! ... you can't 'figure it out!' You know that true poverty—the *pull* of absolute poverty—is
the pull of God's love ... His call to unity ... His invitation to dance!

"So dance! You know the dance—and have always known it. Do it! Whirl like Thérèse … Whirl like me … Whirl like Marthe—*your Beatrice.*… Be a daring soul!"

A tsunami of emotions swamps my mind. I think of Asia, Iraq, India, and Africa. How, in fact, do the parts of my life that I have passed in those places find me here tonight … in Cairo … in this church?

My mind races, but my spirit is calm.

In the picture above the altar, the Clown is still gazing at Thérèse. Now, just for a fleeting moment, his eyes meet mine. His face, usually so distorted with sneering mockery, is serene, his eyes no longer frantic. Suddenly he is gone. I know I will never see him again.

The image of Thérèse fades slowly. Then she, too, is gone. And so are all the circus folk.

The church is almost empty.

I walk in a daze toward the main door. As I am about to push it open I notice her, just inside the door near the baptismal font. It's Sarah Feld.

"Hello, Paul," she says. Her voice has lost its anxious edge.

"Marthe and I were late arriving here and couldn't find seats, so we stood here for Mass. But then she just disappeared."

I shrug. I am not yet ready to describe the past ten minutes of my life to anyone.

Sarah Feld continues.

"Look, Paul, Marthe wants to move the Akbar Club here to Cairo for a while—at least until the bombing stops in Baghdad. Everyone else thinks it's a good idea. They're all in Cairo now. The UN shut its office there, so I'm here, too.

"We all hope you agree, too."

"I agree."

From the corner of my eye I catch a glimpse of Shadow Peirce pushing his way out of the church through the main door. Just as he leaves he turns his head toward me and, jabbing a forefinger in my direction, silently mouths, "You bastard!"

I haven't felt happier in a long, long time.

Sarah Feld speaks again.

"I'm worried about Marthe. Have you seen her?"

"Yes," I reply, "I think we may have just talked."

"Good," Sarah says softly, not pressing me.

She is not looking at me but instead is looking at the water in the baptismal font. She quickly dips her finger into the font.

Then, raising her eyes to mine, she adds, "Marthe told me at the *sema* that she had a special message to give you here. I'm glad you found each other."

Author's Note

Kierkegaard's Clown is a work of fiction. All characters, dialogue, and incidents are either fictitious or used fictitiously. Any resemblance to actual incidents or persons, living or dead, is wholly coincidental and references to actual persons, establishments, organizations, or locales are intended only to convey a sense of authenticity and are used fictitiously. (St. Thérèse's relics visited Iraq in the run-up to the U.S. invasion but were gone before the bombs fell.)

978-0-595-44012-2
0-595-44012-6

Printed in the United States
86093LV00004B/436-501/A